NRA CET - Intermediate Pass

General English

Latest Edition
Practice Kit

12 Tests
12 Topic-Wise Test

Topic Wise Chapters with Questions

✓ Thoroughly Revised and Updated

✓ Detailed Analysis of all MCQs

Title : NRA CET - Intermediate Pass General English
Author Name : Mr. Rohit Manglik
Published By : EduGorilla Community Pvt. Ltd.
Publishers Address : 12/651, First Floor Opp. Arvindo Park, Near Jama Masjid, Indira Nagar, Lucknow, Uttar Pradesh-226016, India

Copyright EduGorilla

ISBN : 978-93-55561-74-9

First Edition

Disclaimer EduGorilla

Compiled and created by EduGorilla Community Pvt. Ltd

Printed By EduGorilla Community Pvt. Ltd.

ROHIT MANGLIK
CEO, EduGorilla

Dear Applicants,

People say *"Success comes to those who work hard."* But I've seen people working hard for their exams day in and day out for marginal success. While others succeed in their examinations by putting in just half the work. So are they God Gifted? No! I believe that it's because they work *smart* and not just *hard*. Similarly, for your exams, you should strategize your preparation so as to increase the likelihood of success. Well with EduGorilla get ready to increase your *chances of selection* in your exam by *16x*.

EduGorilla helps you in not only working *hard* but also working in a *smart and strategic* manner. With EduGorilla's preparation package, you get a chance to make your exam preparation easy, and a fun learning path towards selection. Finding the right path to your preparations can be difficult if you don't know in which direction to head. Don't worry, we have you covered! EduGorilla will be your guide to success in your journey. With our Preparation Package, you can prepare strategically and beat the exam in just one attempt.

EduGorilla's Preparation Package includes-

- **Test Series**
- **Books**

Our preparation package is handcrafted as per the latest changes, expert opinions, and students' discretion. Thus, enabling you to get through each stage of the selection process for your exam.

Our Books are designed by the teachers and experts of the respective exam with a combined 150+ years of experience; to provide you with easy, efficient, and effective learning. Our books are smart, in the sense that not only do they give you the answers to the questions but also provide similar questions for practice.

EduGorilla's competent Test Series gives you real-time experience and confidence through which you can clear your offline or online exam in just one attempt. We currently host 83,000+ mock tests for 1,440+ competitive and academic exams.

Thus, EduGorilla misses no chance to assist you in your preparation and covers all stages of the exam, so that you don't have to look anywhere else.

We provide complete preparation packages for defense, banking, teaching, and other National & State-Level exams. Hence, it doesn't matter which exam you aspire to because you will reach your success.

ALL THE BEST !

Let EduGorilla be your Guide to Success.

Rohit Manglik,
Founder and CEO, EduGorilla

Editor's Note

INTRODUCTION

EduGorilla focuses on guiding students to succeed in their examinations. With that in mind, our book, titled "NRA CET - Intermediate Pass : General English", has been drafted through the collective efforts of our distinguished experts with 150+ years of combined experience. This book consists of questions that are created following the latest changes in the syllabus and exam pattern. We compiled the book on the basis of questions that are most likely to appear in the . Through EduGorilla's "NRA CET - Intermediate Pass : General English" your chances of success will increase 16x.

EduGorilla does this through our Complete Preparation Package. This package consists of well-conceptualized and structured content in the form of questions that are tailor-made according to your needs and will help you practice for exams in a smart way by pinpointing all the necessary information. It also provides hints and solutions, along with a smart answer sheet for your self-evaluation. You can assess your shortcomings and work accordingly on areas that may require more of your attention.

EduGorilla promises to help you succeed in your examination and accomplish your dream goals. We believe in our aspirants and see them at the top of the merit list. And the first step towards the top is to start preparing with us. EduGorilla's "NRA CET - Intermediate Pass : General English" includes the following attributes.

➤ Well-Researched Content

➤ Top-Notch Quality

➤ Detailed Answers and Analysis

➤ Smart Answer Sheet

➤ Exam Relevant Questions

Therefore, EduGorilla fortifies your preparation and makes it durable enough to help you stand tall and beat the examination.

TABLE OF CONTENTS

Ques (1-30):Direction: Choose the option that is the correct active/passive form of the sentence.

Q.1 They are doing a great work by helping the poor.
A. A great work is being done by them by helping the poor
B. Helping the poor is a great work
C. A great work had been done by them by helping the poor
D. A great work was done by them by helping the poor

Q.2 We all regard Liza as an expert.
A. Liza has been regarded as an expert by all of us.
B. Liza was regarded as an expert by all of us.
C. Liza is regarded as an expert by all of us.
D. Liza should be regarded as an expert by all of us.

Q.3 We have looked at the plan carefully.
A. The plan was carefully looked at.
B. The plan is being carefully looked at.
C. The plan have been carefully looked at.
D. The plan has been carefully looked at.

Q.4 By whom were you pushed into the mud?
A. Whom did you push into the mud?
B. Who pushed you into the mud?
C. Who has pushed you into the mud?
D. Who was pushing you into the mud?

Q.5 They will lay the foundation stone next week.
A. The foundation stone is being laid by them next week.
B. The foundation stone will be laying by next week.
C. The foundation stone will be laid by them next week.
D. The foundation stone will have been laid by them next week.

Q.6 Was your bag left in the bus?
A. Did you left your bag in the bus?
B. Was you leaving your bag in the bus?
C. Have you left your bag in the bus?
D. Did you leave your bag in the bus?

Q.7 The catch should not be dropped.
A. Have you dropped the catch?
B. Let the catch not be dropped.
C. You would not drop the catch.
D. Don't drop the catch.

Q.8 The politician's speech was loudly cheered.
A. The audience cheer the politician's loud speech.
B. The audience was loudly cheered by the politician's speech.
C. The audience loudly cheered the politician's speech.
D. The audience had been loudly cheered by the politician.

Q.9 They considered it an impressive building.
A. It was considered to be an impressive building.
B. It can be consider to be an impressive building.
C. It was considering to being an impressive building.
D. It is considered to be an impressive building.

Q.10 They found her guilty of theft.
A. She found them guilty of theft.
B. She was found guilty of theft.
C. She had been find guilty of theft.
D. She is find guilty of theft by them.

Q.11 The security guard opened the gate using his pass.
A. The gate is open by the security guard by using his pass.
B. The gate was opened by the security guard using his pass.
C. The gate opened the security guard using his pass.
D. The gate was open by the security guard use his pass.

Q.12 The first settlers displaced the original inhabitants.
A. The original inhabitants are displacing the first settlers.
B. The original inhabitants were displaced by the first settlers.
C. The original inhabitants will displace the first settlers.
D. The original inhabitants are being displace by the first settlers.

Q.13 Who helped you with your homework?
A. By who was you helped with your homework?
B. By whom were you helped with your homework?
C. Your homework was helped by whom?
D. Who had helped you with your homework?

Q.14 A children's story is written by Amith.
[SSC Sub Inspector (CPO), 2018], [SSC Sub Inspector (CPO), 2017]
A. Amith has written a children's story.
B. Amith wrote a children's story.
C. Amith writes a children's story.
D. Amith had written a children's story.

Q.15 The books exhibition had been opened by the Governor.
[SSC Sub Inspector (CPO), 2018], [SSC Sub Inspector (CPO), 2017]
A. The Governor had opened the books exhibition.
B. The Governor has opened the books exhibition.
C. The Governor opened the books exhibition.
D. The Governor opens the books exhibition.

Q.16 He was taken to the hospital by his friends.
[SSC Sub Inspector (CPO), 2018], [SSC Sub Inspector (CPO), 2017]
A. His friends had taken him to the hospital.
B. His friends have taken him to the hospital.
C. His friends take him to the hospital.
D. His friends took him to the hospital.

Q.17 A gift was given to me by my friend.
[SSC Sub Inspector (CPO), 2018], [SSC Sub Inspector (CPO), 2017]
A. My friend had given me a gift.

B. My friend has given me a gift.
C. My friend gave me a gift.
D. My friend gives me a gift.

Q.18 The invitation cards will be sent today.
A. They will sent the invitation cards today.
B. They will have sent the invitation cards today.
C. They will send the invitation cards today.
D. They will be sending the invitation cards today.

Q.19 How much a month are you paid?
A. How much a month do you pay?
B. In a month how much do you pay?
C. How much a month do they pay you?
D. How much a month do you pay the?

Q.20 Who taught you to dance?
A. Who did teach you to dance?
B. By who were you taught to dance?
C. You were taught to dance by who?
D. By whom were you taught to dance?

Q.21 Your mother called you many times.
A. You was called many times by your mother.
B. You were being called many times by your mother.
C. You called many times by your mother.
D. You were called many times by your mother.

Q.22 They were playing hockey in the garden.
A. Hockey is being played by them in the garden.
B. Hockey was played by them in the garden.
C. Hockey were being played by them in the garden.
D. Hockey was being played by them in the garden.

Q.23 Call the police.
A. Let the police be called.
B. Let us be called by the police.
C. The police be called by you.
D. We are calling the police.

Q.24 An online order has been placed by me today.
A. I placed an online order today.
B. I have placed an online order today.
C. I am placing an online order today.
D. I will place an online order today.

Q.25 So much noise ought not to be made by you and your friends
A. You and your friends ought to not make so much noise.
B. You and your friends ought not to have made so much noise.
C. You and your friends ought not to be making so much noise.
D. You and your friends ought not to make so much noise.

Q.26 Rahul is playing cricket in the playground provided by the government.
A. Cricket is played by Rahul in the playground provided by the government.
B. Cricket has been played by Rahul in the playground provided by the government.
C. Cricket is been played by Rahul in the playground provided by the government.
D. Cricket is being played by Rahul in the playground provided by the government.

Q.27 A complaint has been made by him against the poor service of the hotel staff.
A. He had made a complaint against the poor service of the hotel staff.
B. He will make a complaint against the poor service of the hotel staff.
C. He has made a complaint against the poor service of the hotel staff.
D. He is making a complaint against the poor service of the hotel staff.

Q.28 The light was switched off by her before sleeping.
A. She switches off the light before sleeping.
B. She is switching off the light before sleeping.
C. She had switched off the light before sleeping.
D. She switched off the light before sleeping.

Q.29 He will surely be elected by the people in the next elections.
A. People would surely be electing him in the next election.
B. He will surely elect the people in the next election.
C. People will surely be electing him in the next election.
D. People will surely elect him in the next election.

Q.30 The hunchback was being laughed at by everyone
A. Everyone is laughing at the hunchback
B. Everyone laughs at the hunchback
C. Everyone laughed at the hunchback
D. Everyone was laughing at the hunchback

// Smart Answer Sheet //

Correct — Indicates percentage of students who answered questions correctly.

Skipped — Indicates percentage of students who skipped questions.

Q.	Ans.	Correct	Skipped
1	A	65.11 %	33.66 %
2	C	46.7 %	51.13 %
3	D	66.95 %	31.52 %
4	B	59.26 %	39.21 %
5	C	56.08 %	38.98 %
6	D	57.62 %	35.39 %
7	D	63.7 %	35.81 %
8	C	69.66 %	30.01 %
9	A	63.53 %	31.16 %
10	B	50.69 %	41.81 %
11	B	46.51 %	37.21 %
12	B	68.95 %	30.87 %
13	B	41.28 %	43.44 %
14	C	49.2 %	47.71 %
15	A	67.05 %	31.65 %
16	D	63.86 %	34.41 %
17	C	44.86 %	35.1 %
18	C	42.22 %	44.79 %
19	C	49.19 %	33.01 %
20	D	66.74 %	32.23 %
21	D	63.38 %	32.6 %
22	D	62.18 %	35.32 %
23	A	56.55 %	35.46 %
24	B	57.72 %	33.5 %
25	D	51.81 %	45.7 %
26	D	68.08 %	30.38 %
27	C	45.11 %	38.06 %
28	D	43.47 %	56.1 %
29	D	48.81 %	39.29 %
30	D	58.72 %	33.32 %

Performance Analysis	
Avg. Score (%)	36.67%
Toppers Score (%)	70.0%
Your Score	

//Hints and Solutions//

1. The given sentence is in the active voice. Its tense is present continuous. The structures for active/passive voices are:

Active: Subject + is/are/am + verb (ing) + object.

Passive: Object + is/are/am + being + verb (IIIrd from) + by + subject.

So, with the help of the above structures, we can convert the given sentence into passive voice:

A great work is being done by them by helping the poor.

Hence, the correct option is (A).

2. In Passive Voice, a sentence emphasizes the action or the object of the sentence. The given sentence is in the active voice and 'We' is the subject and 'Liza' is the object.

When we convert this sentence into passive voice, the subject 'We' of the active voice becomes the object 'us', the object 'Liza' becomes the subject. The passive format "is + V_3 (regarded)" should be used.

Passive form- Liza is regarded as an expert by all of us.

Hence, the correct option is (C).

3. The structure of the given sentence is as follows:

- Subject (Objective Case)+has/have+been+V_3+Object (Subjective Case). (Passive Voice)
- 'The plan' will be put in place of 'we'. (Subject becomes object)
- And 'we' will be put in place of 'the plan'. (The object becomes subject)
- 'Have looked at' will be changed into 'has looked at'. (To agree with the changed subject and object)

Passive form: 'The plan has been carefully looked at.'

Hence, the correct option is (D).

4. The structure of the given sentence is as follows:

- Who+V_2+Subject+Object? (Active Voice)
- 'By whom' will be changed into 'who' (Object becomes subject).
- 'Were' will be removed. (Passive -> Active)
- 'into the mud' will be written as it is.

Active form: 'Who pushed you into the mud?'

Hence, the correct option is (B).

5. The process of transformation is as follows:

- The subject of the given sentence is 'They'.
- The object of the given sentence is 'the foundation'.
- The subject will be put in place of the object and the object will be put in place of the subject.
- 'Will lay' will be changed into 'will be laid' (subject-verb agreement).

Passive form: 'The foundation stone will be laid by them next week.'

Hence, the correct option is (C).

6. We need to follow these instructions while changing the voice of an interrogative sentence.

The inverted form of the verb i.e., did you leave, will commence the sentence.

The given sentence is in the simple past tense.

The active voice form for the simple past interrogative sentence: Helping verb (Did) + subject + V_1 + object?

Active form: 'Did you leave your bag in the bus?'

Hence, the correct option is (D).

7. An imperative sentence does not normally have a subject. It is used to express a command or request. The imperative sentence in the active and passive voice takes the following form:

V_1 + Object.

Object + should be + V_3.

Example: Help the needy. (Active Voice)

Active form: 'Don't drop the catch.'

Hence, the correct option is (D).

8. In the active form, the subject and the object will get interchanged. So, 'the politician's speech' will become the object. The passive form contains 'was' which means the active form must be in the past tense.

Option (A) is in the present tense.

Option (B) changes the meaning.

Option (D) is in the past perfect tense.

Rules of Conversion from Passive to Active Voice:

- Identify the subject, the verb and the object: S+V+O.
- Change the subject into object.
- Omit the suitable helping verb or auxiliary verb.
- Change the past participle to simple past tense form of the verb.
- Omit the preposition "by".
- Change the object into subject.

The correct answer is: 'The audience loudly cheered the politician's speech.'

Hence, the correct option is (C).

9. The following steps are required to change the given sentence into passive voice:

In the passive form, the subject and the object will be interchanged. 'It' will become the subject.

The tense(simple past tense) will change according to the following structure:

- Active Voice - Subject + did + V_1 or V_2 + Object.

- Passive Voice - Object + was/were + V_3 + by + Object.

Option (B) and (D) are in the present tense.

Option (C) is in the past continuous tense.

The correct answer is: We need to change it in the passive voice.

Hence, the correct option is (A).

10. The voice of a verb tells whether the subject of the sentence performs or receives the action.

In active voice, the subject (agent) acts upon the verb; while in passive, the verb acts upon the subject (agent).

Rules of Conversion from Active to Passive Voice:

- Identify the subject, the verb and the object: S+V+O.
- Change the object into subject.
- Put the suitable helping verb or auxiliary verb.
- Change the verb into past participle of the verb.
- Add the preposition "by".
- Change the subject into object.

Option (B) follows all the proper conversion rules.

The correct answer is: She was found guilty of theft.

Hence, the correct option is (B).

11. The following steps are required to change the given sentence into passive voice:

The subject 'the security guard' of the active voice will become the object of the passive voice.

The object 'the gate' of the active voice will become the subject of the passive voice.

The tense (simple past tense) will change according to the following structure:-

Active Voice - Subject + did + V_1 or V_2 + Object.

Passive Voice - Object + was/were + V_3 + by + Object.

Thus, 'opened' will be converted to 'was opened'.

The correct answer is: The gate was opened by the security guard using his pass.

Hence, the correct option is (B).

12. The following steps are required to change the given sentence into passive voice:

The subject 'the first settlers' of the active voice will become the object of the passive voice.

The object 'the original inhabitants' of the active voice will become the subject of the passive voice.

The tense(simple past tense) will change according to the following structure:

- Active Voice - Subject + did + V_1 or V_2 + Object.
- Passive Voice - Object + was/were + V_3 + by + Object.

Thus, 'displaced' will be converted to 'were displaced'.

The correct answer is: The original inhabitants were displaced by the first settlers.

Hence, the correct option is (B).

13. For simple past sentences that start with "who", the following structures are followed for active/passive voice:
Active: Who + verb (IInd form) + object?

Passive: By whom + was/were + object + verb (IIIrd form)?

So, the passive sentence would be:

By whom were you helped with your homework?

Hence, the correct option is (B).

14. We need to follow these instructions while changing the voice of an assertive sentence:

Find the subject and object of the sentence and exchange their places; make changes in their cases as well if subject and object are pronouns.

The proposition 'by' is removed in the active voice.

If 'is/ am/ are + v_3' is used in the passive voice, the sentence in the active voice will be in the present indefinite tense.

In the present indefinite tense 'v_1 + s/es' is used. Hence, 'writes' will be used.

At last line up the remaining part.

The correct sentence is: Amith writes a children's story.

Hence, the correct option is (C).

15. We need to follow these instructions while changing the voice of an assertive sentence:

The given sentence is in passive form.

Find the subject and object of the sentence and exchange their places; make changes in their cases as well if subject and object are pronouns.

If 'had been + V_3' is used in the passive form, 'had + V_3' will be used in the active form (had opened).

Remove the preposition 'by' in the active form.

At last line up the remaining part.

The correct sentence is: The Governor had opened the books exhibition.

Hence, the correct option is (A).

16. We need to follow these instructions while changing the voice of an assertive sentence:

The given sentence is in passive form.

Find the subject and object of the sentence and exchange their places; make changes in their cases as well if subject and object are pronouns.

If 'was/were + V_3' is used in the passive form, then change the sentence to simple past tense (V_2 - took) in the active form.

Remove the preposition 'by' in the active form.

At last line up the remaining part.

The correct sentence is: His friends took him to the hospital.

Hence, the correct option is (D).

17. We need to follow these instructions while changing the voice of an assertive sentence:

- The given sentence is in passive form.
- Find the subject and object of the sentence and exchange their places; make changes in their cases as well if subject and object are pronouns.
- If 'was/were + V_3' is used in the passive form, then change the sentence to simple past tense (V_2 - gave) in the active form.
- Remove the preposition 'by' in the active form.
- At last line up the remaining part.

The correct sentence is: My friend gave me a gift.

Hence, the correct option is (C).

18. The given sentence is in the passive voice of simple future tense. Let us understand the structures for active/passive voices for such sentences.

Active: Subject + will/shall + verb (Ist form) + object.

Passive: Object + will/shall + be + verb (IIIrd form) + by + subject.

So, with the help of the above structures, we can convert the sentence into active voice:

They will send the invitation cards today.

Hence, the correct option is (C).

19. The given sentence is in a passive form of present interrogative tense. The structures for active/passive voices are:

Active: Question word + do/does + subject + verb (Ist form) + object?

Passive: Question word + is/are/am + object + verb (IIIrd from) + by + subject?

So, with the help of the above structures, we can convert the given sentence into active voice:

How much a month do they pay you?

Hence, the correct option is (C).

20. The given sentence is of past interrogative tense that starts with "who". The structures for active/passive for such sentences are:

Active: Who + verb (IInd form) + object?

Passive: By whom + was/were + verb (IIIrd form) + object?

So, the passive sentence would be:

By whom were you taught to dance?

Hence, the correct option is (D).

21. The given sentence is in the active form of simple past tense. The structures for active/passive voices are:
Active: Subject + verb (IInd form) + object.

Passive: Object + was/were + verb (IIIrd form) + by + subject.

So, with the help of the above structures, we can convert the given sentence into passive voice:

You were called many times by your mother.

Hence, the correct option is (D).

22. The given sentence is in the active voice. Its tense is past continuous. The structures for active/passive voices are:

Active: Subject + was/were + verb (ing) + object.

Passive: Object + was/were + being + verb (IIIrd from) + by + subject.

So, with the help of the above structures, we can convert the given sentence into passive voice:

Hockey was being played by them in the garden.

Hence, the correct option is (D).

23. The passive voice of imperative sentences that suggest order, suggestion, or request can be made in two ways:

Active: Verb + object

Passive: Let + object + be + past participle

You are requested/ordered/suggested + to + verb (I^{st} form) + object

So, the passive voice of the given sentence would be:

Let the police be called.

Or

You are requested to call the police.

Since the first type is given in option A, it is the correct answer.

Hence, the correct option is (A).

24. When we convert this sentence into active voice, the subject 'An online' of the passive voice becomes the object, the object 'me' becomes the subject 'I'.

The passive format "has + been + V3 (placed)" should be converted into the active format "have + V2 (placed)" to account for the new subject-verb agreement

This is the active and passive voice rule for the present perfect tense.

The correct sentence is: I have placed an online order today.

Hence, the correct option is (B).

25. The given sentence is an imperative one and in the passive voice form.

Follow the active form structure for the modals given above:

Exchange the places of the subject and object. (So much noise - you and your friends)

Now the modal verb will be used followed by the 1st form of the verb. (ought not to make)

At last, line up the remaining part.

The correct sentence is: You and your friends ought not to make so much noise.

Hence, the correct option is (D).

26. Whenever a sentence in present continuous tense is changed into its passive voice, then we follow the given structure:-

'Is/am/are + Ving' is changed to 'is/am/are + being + V3'.

For Example:-

Active - They are playing cricket in that field.

Passive - Cricket is being played by them in that field.

Therefore, the correct passive voice of the given sentence is 'Cricket is being played by Rahul in the playground provided by the government'.

Hence, the correct option is (D).

27. The given sentence is in Passive Voice. As per the given question we have to change it into Active Voice.

The structure of the given sentence as follows:

Subject+has/have+V3+Object. (Active Voice)

Subject (Objective Case)+has/have+V3+Object (Subjective Case). (Passive Voice)

'Him' will be changed into 'He'. (Object will become Subject)

'A complaint' will be put in place of 'Him'. (Subject will become Object)

'Has been made' will be changed into 'has made'.

'The poor service of the hotel staff' will be written as it is.

The correct sentence is: He has made a complaint against the poor service of the hotel staff.

Hence, the correct option is (C).

28. The given sentence is in the passive voice and 'The light' is the subject and 'her' is the object.

When we convert this sentence into active voice, the subject 'The light' of the passive voice becomes the object, the object 'her' becomes the subject 'she'.

The passive format "was + V3 (switched)" should be changed into the active format "switched".

This is the active and passive voice rule for the past simple tense.

The correct sentence is: She switched off the light before sleeping.

Hence, the correct option is (D).

29. The given sentence is in Passive Voice. As per the given question we have to change it into Active Voice.

The process of transformation as follows:

The subject of the given sentence is 'He'.

The object of the given sentence is 'the people'.

The subject will be put in place of the object and the object will be put in place of the subject.

'will surely be elected' will be changed into 'will surely elect'.

The rest of the sentence will be written as it is.

The correct sentence is: People will surely elect him in the next election.

Hence, the correct option is (D).

30. The given sentence is in the passive voice and 'The hunchback' is the subject and 'everyone' is the object.

When we convert this sentence into active voice, the subject 'The hunchback' of the passive voice becomes the object, the object 'everyone' becomes the subject.

The passive format "was + being + V3" is used and the active format "was + ing" should be used.

This is the active and passive voice rule for the past continuous tense.

The correct sentence is: "Everyone was laughing at the hunchback".

Hence, the correct option is (D).

Ques (1-10):Direction: In the following passage, there are blanks, each of which has been numbered. Choose the correct word from the given options which fits the blank appropriately.

_(1)_ October 12, 1492, the Italian _(2)_ Christopher Columbus landed on a small island in the Caribbean, which he named San Salvador and claimed for Spain, the country that had _(3)_ his voyage. _(4)_ Columbus was not actually the first European to reach the Americas, and millions of indigenous people already lived there, he has traditionally been _(5)_ in the United States as the "discoverer" of the Americas. The first Columbus Day _(6)_ took place _(7)_ 1792 the 300th anniversary of his _(8)_. Columbus Day celebrations _(9)_ in popularity over the decades that followed, especially in Italian American and other Catholic immigrant communities, where amid a general climate of anti-Catholic prejudice, Columbus was _(10)_ as a symbol of what it meant to be both Catholic and American. A federal holiday was signed into law by Franklin Delano Roosevelt in 1937.

Q.1 Which of the following words most appropriately fits the blank numbered _(1)_?

[SSC Sub Inspector (CPO), 2018]

A. on **B.** in **C.** at **D.** to

Q.2 Which of the following words most appropriately fits the blank numbered _(2)_?

[SSC Sub Inspector (CPO), 2018]

A. inventor **B.** scientist
C. explorer **D.** shipwright

Q.3 Which of the following words most appropriately fits the blank numbered _(3)_?

[SSC Sub Inspector (CPO), 2018]

A. enemy **B.** sponsored
C. boycotted **D.** competitor

Q.4 Which of the following words most appropriately fits the blank numbered _(4)_?

[SSC Sub Inspector (CPO), 2018]

A. through **B.** because **C.** for **D.** although

Q.5 Which of the following words most appropriately fits the blank numbered _(5)_?

[SSC Sub Inspector (CPO), 2018]

A. celebrated **B.** hated
C. ignored **D.** unexalted

Q.6 Which of the following words most appropriately fits the blank numbered _(6)_?

A. function **B.** celebration
C. performance **D.** purpose

Q.7 Which of the following words most appropriately fits the blank numbered _(7)_?

A. to **B.** on **C.** at **D.** in

Q.8 Which of the following words most appropriately fits the blank numbered _(8)_?

[SSC Sub Inspector (CPO), 2018]

A. departure **B.** exit
C. arrival **D.** meeting

Q.9 Which of the following words most appropriately fits the blank numbered _(9)_?

[SSC Sub Inspector (CPO), 2018]

A. grew **B.** growing **C.** grown **D.** grows

Q.10 Which of the following words most appropriately fits the blank numbered _(10)_?

[SSC Sub Inspector (CPO), 2018]

A. regarded **B.** neglected
C. scorned **D.** regarding

Ques (11-20):Direction: In the following passage, some of the words have been left out. Read the passage carefully and select the correct answer out of the four alternatives for the given blanks.

The other day I visited a refugee _____ (1) where the victims _____ (2) the Gujarat Earthquake _____ (3) in very_____ (4) conditions. I was particularly _____ (5) by an old woman who was determined to give _____ (6) grandchildren a better future. She _____ (7) a strong and _____ (8) woman who even after the _____ (9) of her own children undertook such a journey through life and never felt weak or broken but was an _____ (10) for all.

Q.11 Find out the appropriate word for the case 1.

A. House **B.** Camp **C.** Home **D.** Nest

Q.12 Find out the appropriate word for the case 2.

A. Of **B.** To **C.** In **D.** At

Q.13 Find out the appropriate word for the case 3.

A. Was living **B.** Are living
C. Were living **D.** Have lived

Q.14 Find out the appropriate word for the case 4.

A. Apathetic **B.** Sympathetic
C. Pathetic **D.** Empathetic

Q.15 Find out the appropriate word for the case 5.

A. Cornered **B.** Collected
C. Worked **D.** Moved

Q.16 Find out the appropriate word for the case 6.

A. His **B.** Her **C.** Its **D.** Their

Q.17 Find out the appropriate word for the case 7.

A. Were **B.** Had **C.** Was **D.** Is

Q.18 Find out the appropriate word for the case 8.

A. Courageous
B. Continuous
C. Ruinous
D. Careful

Q.19 Find out the appropriate word for the case 9.

A. Life
B. Death
C. Motionless
D. Captivated

Q.20 Find out the appropriate word for the case 10.

A. Happiness
B. Determination
C. Motivation
D. Inspiration

Ques (21-30):Direction: In the following passage, some of the words have been left out. Read the passage carefully and select the correct answer out of the four alternatives for the given blanks.

The wings of some birds are so small that they are _____ (1) for flying. Earlier such birds _____ (2) fly but after living for thousands of _____ (3) in places where they had no _____ (4) there was no need for them to fly and they _____ (5) on the ground. After a while, their _____ (6) ones could no longer rise into the air. The ostrich, rhea, emu and cassowary _____ (7) fly, but they can run fast on their long and strong legs. Ostriches _____ (8) in Africa and are found on the grassy places _____ (9) they live along with big groups of zebras. The rhea looks like the ostrich _____ (10) it is smaller and has three toes on each foot, while the ostrich has only two.

Q.21 Find out the appropriate word for the case 1.

A. Useless
B. Useful
C. Beneficial
D. Suited

Q.22 Find out the appropriate word for the case 2.

A. Should B. Might C. Could D. Can

Q.23 Find out the appropriate word for the case 3.

A. Weeks B. Years C. Months D. Ages

Q.24 Find out the appropriate word for the case 4.

A. Wind B. Sky C. Friends D. Enemies

Q.25 Find out the appropriate word for the case 5.

A. Stepped B. Stayed C. Crept D. Crawled

Q.26 Find out the appropriate word for the case 6.

A. Trained B. Old C. Young D. Pregnant

Q.27 Find out the appropriate word for the case 7.

A. Cannot B. Could C. Would D. Should

Q.28 Find out the appropriate word for the case 8.

A. Lived
B. Live
C. Had lived
D. Used to live

Q.29 Find out the appropriate word for the case 9.

A. When B. Where C. So that D. Because

Q.30 Find out the appropriate word for the case 10.

A. Even though
B. But
C. And
D. In spite of

// Smart Answer Sheet //

Correct Indicates percentage of students who answered questions correctly.

Skipped Indicates percentage of students who skipped questions.

Q.	Ans.	Correct	Skipped
1	A	49.28 %	50.38 %
2	C	50.62 %	41.56 %
3	B	54.72 %	39.19 %
4	D	45.9 %	47.35 %
5	A	50.22 %	32.43 %
6	B	66.64 %	32.7 %
7	D	68.56 %	31.08 %
8	C	45.54 %	31.88 %
9	A	57.25 %	30.69 %
10	A	65.29 %	32.76 %
11	B	68.06 %	30.05 %
12	A	45.33 %	43.89 %
13	C	60.06 %	34.34 %
14	C	62.58 %	30.15 %
15	D	49.25 %	39.37 %
16	B	65.22 %	31.54 %
17	C	68.06 %	31.31 %
18	A	43.07 %	35.81 %
19	B	44.74 %	30.14 %
20	D	69.11 %	30.63 %
21	A	69.95 %	30.04 %
22	C	48.11 %	47.25 %
23	B	41.65 %	32.9 %
24	D	64.7 %	34.51 %
25	B	60.7 %	39.12 %
26	C	59.43 %	32.05 %
27	A	53.5 %	32.03 %
28	B	68.81 %	30.05 %
29	B	45.22 %	48.86 %
30	B	63.13 %	31.17 %

Performance Analysis	
Avg. Score (%)	46.67%
Toppers Score (%)	56.67%
Your Score	

//Hints and Solutions//

1. The correct sentence is - On October 12, 1492, the Italian explorer Christopher Columbus landed on a small island in the Caribbean.

On is used with specific days of the week or year. –on 1st of Jan / on Monday.

At is used with specific times of the day/ with specific places in a city. – at school / at 12 o'clock.

To is used with verbs to show movement such as go and come.—to school.

In is used with months of the year/ seasons / countries.—in April / in Summer.

A date begins the passage-- so the obvious word fit for the blank is 'on'.

Hence, the correct option is (A).

2. The correct sentence is- On October 12, 1492, the Italian **explorer** Christopher Columbus landed on a small island in the Caribbean.

Explorer means a person who explores a new or unfamiliar area.

Inventor means one who devises something new.

Scientist means an expert in science.

Shipwright means a shipbuilder.

The sentence is about Christopher Columbus, so the correct word is ' **explorer**'.

Hence, the correct option is (C).

3. The correct sentence is- Christopher Columbus landed on a small island in the Caribbean, which he named San Salvador and claimed for Spain, the country that had **sponsored** his voyage.

Sponsored means to support a person, organization, or activity by giving money.

Enemy means a person who hates or opposes another person.

Boycotted means to refuse to buy or handle (goods) as a punishment or protest.

Competitor means a person who takes part in a sporting contest.

The sentence is about an explorer who had been sponsored by his country to explore the world. So the right word is '**sponsored**'.

Hence, the correct option is (B).

4. The correct sentence is -- Although Columbus was not actually the first European to reach the Americas he was known as the discoverer of the Americas.

Although means in spite of the fact that.

Through is used to show from one end or side of something to the other.

Because means for the reason that.

For refers to because of or as a result of something.

The given sentence is about Christopher Columbus, and this is giving more information about the same.

Hence, the correct option is (D).

5. The correct sentence is - Although Columbus was not actually the first European to reach the Americas and millions of indigenous people already lived there, he has traditionally been **celebrated** in the United States as the discoverer of the Americas.

Celebrated means greatly admired; renowned.

Hated means disliked by many people.

Ignored means to give no attention to something.

Unexalted means uninspired.

Hence, the correct option is (A).

6. The right sentence is- The first Columbus Day **celebration** took place in 1792 the 300th anniversary of his arrival.

Celebration means to mark a special day, event, or holiday.

Function means an official ceremony.

Performance means a musical, dramatic, or other entertainment presented before an audience.

Purpose means the reason for which something is done.

Hence, the correct option is (B).

7. The correct sentence is - The first Columbus Day celebration took place **in** 1792 the 300th anniversary of his arrival.

To /At / On / In are all prepositions used for different purposes.

- **In** is used to show location.
- **To** is used to show movement towards something.
- **On** is used for specific dates and to show the surface of something.
- **At** is used for a specific time or place.

Hence, the correct option is (D).

8. The correct sentence is --The first Columbus Day celebration took place in 1792 the 300th anniversary of his **arrival**.

Arrival is the act of coming to or reaching a place.

Departure is the act of going away from somewhere.

Exit is an act of leaving a place.

A **meeting** is when people come together to discuss something.

Hence, the correct option is (C).

9. The correct sentence is--Columbus Day celebrations **grew** in popularity over the decades that followed, especially in Italian American and other Catholic immigrant communities.

Grew is the past tense of grow, means to increase in size or amount.

Growing is the continuous tense of grow.

Grown is the past participle of grow.

Grows is the is the third person present tense of grow.

Since the sentence is in the past tense, the verb too should be in the past tense.

Hence, the correct option is (A).

10. The correct sentence thus is - Columbus was **regarded** as a symbol of what it meant to be both Catholic and American.

Regarded means to be thought of in a specified way.

Neglected means disregarded.

Scorned means to feel or express contempt or disdain for someone.

Regarding means concerning.

Hence, the correct option is (A).

11. The given passage talks about a scenario after the Gujarat Earthquake. At such places, the government set up refugee camps for the victims to stay there. Words like "home, house or nest" cannot be used in this scenario.

Hence, the correct option is (B).

12. The correct preposition to be used in the sentence is "of" as it connects the relationship of the victims to the Gujarat Earthquakes.

Hence, the correct option is (A).

13. The given passage describes a past scenario. Therefore, only past tense can be used here. Since the subject is "victims" which is plural in case, it should also carry a plural verb.

Hence, the correct option is (C).

14. In order to find the correct word, let's understand their meanings first:

Apathetic = showing or feeling no interest, enthusiasm, or concern.

Sympathetic = feeling, showing, or expressing sympathy.

Pathetic = arousing pity, especially through vulnerability or sadness.

Empathetic = showing an ability to understand and share the feelings of another.

The passage describes a scenario where the author was feeling pity and sadness at the condition of the earthquake victims. So, the correct emotions are described by the adjective "pathetic".

Hence, the correct option is (C).

15. The author mentions a woman who though being old was determined to give her children a bright future. The correct phrasal verb here is "to be moved by" which means to have strong feelings of sadness or sympathy because of something someone has said or done.

Hence, the correct option is (D).

16. We need a pronoun to show the relationship between the grandmother and her children. Therefore, the correct pronoun is "her".

Hence, the correct option is (B).

17. The given sentence describes the quality of the woman. Since, the reference is of past tense and the woman is a singular noun, the correct helping verb is "was".

Hence, the correct option is (C).

18. The sentence describes the quality of the woman. She cared about the future of her grandchildren even at the time of such disaster and was never afraid of the circumstances. So, the correct adjective to reflect her qualities is "courageous".

Hence, the correct option is (A).

19. The Gujarat Earthquake caused the death of a lot of people. The passage gives the sense that the lady lost her children also in the disaster. So, the word "death" best conveys the required meaning in the sentence.

Hence, the correct option is (B).

20. The correct word here is "inspiration" as the perseverance of the grandmother inspired the author and many other people. She denied feeling weak or broken even after losing her relatives in the calamity.

Hence, the correct option is (D).

21. The sentence talks about some birds whose wings are very small. So, the word in the bracket would show the result of the wings being too small. The correct word is "useless".

Hence, the correct option is (A).

22. These birds were, however, able to fly in the earlier days and they had big wings then. So, the sentence here shows the possibility of the birds' flying. The correct verb, therefore, is "could".

Hence, the correct option is (C).

23. A long time is often measured in years and hence the correct answer is option (B). Weeks and months are incorrect as they are used to refer to a short time ago. Ages is incorrect as it is an uncountable noun and cannot be used with "thousands".

Hence, the correct option is (B).

24. To stay away from their enemies the birds usually fly but in those times these birds did not have any enemy and hence no flying was required.

Hence, the correct option is (D).

25. Since there was no fear of enemies these birds stayed on the ground without trying to fly away. The correct answer is option (B). "Stepped" is an incorrect word and "crept" or "crawled" is used for reptiles like snakes, alligators.

Hence, the correct option is (B).

26. Since children of these birds were raised in a system that required them to stay on ground, these children couldn't learn to fly. To refer to the children of someone, we use the word "young ones".

Hence, the correct option is (C).

27. The sentence is mentioning the ability of certain birds to fly. Birds such as ostrich, emu etc. can't fly since they've become land birds by evolution.

Hence, the correct option is (A).

28. The sentence mentions the natural habitat of the bird named Ostrich which is Africa. Since the sentence is of simple present, the use of any other verb apart from present tense would be incorrect.

Hence, the correct option is (B).

29. The adverb 'where' refers to in or to what place or position. The word "where" is referring to the grassy places of Africa. So, it is the correct answer.

Hence, the correct option is (B).

30. The conjunction 'but' is used to introduce a clause contrasting with what has already been said. The sentence first draws a similarity between Ostrich and Rhea and it also mentions how they are different to each other. So, the use of contrasting conjunction "but" would be correct.

Hence, the correct option is (B).

Q.1 Direction: Choose the option that is the indirect form of the sentence.

Lokesh said, "I am very busy this week".

A. Lokesh said that I am very busy this week.
B. Lokesh said that I am very busy that week.
C. Lokesh said that he was very busy that week.
D. Lokesh said that he are very busy this week.

Q.2 Direction: Choose the option that is the indirect form of the sentence.

"We are going to Tirupati next week," Deepa told her friends.

A. Deepa told her friends that they will go to Tirupati next week.
B. Deepa told to her friends that she is going to Tirupati following week.
C. Deepa told her friends that we were going to Tirupati the following week.
D. Deepa told her friends that they were going to Tirupati the following week.

Q.3 Direction: Choose the option that is the direct form of the sentence.

The Principal said to them that he did not want to see any one to return with a complaint against them.

A. The Principal said to them, "I did not want to saw any one to return with a complaint against them."
B. The Principal said to them, "I do not want to see any one to return with a complaint against you."
C. The Principal said to them, "I do not wanted to see any of them to be returning with a complaint."
D. The Principal said to them, "I do not want to see any one to returns with a complaint against you."

Q.4 Direction: Choose the option that is the indirect form of the sentence.

"Please bring me a cup of coffee," Shakila said to the waiter.

A. Shakila told the waiter to bring her a cup of coffee.
B. Shakila said to the waiter he should bring her a cup of coffee.
C. Shakila told to the waiter that he should brought her a cup of coffee.
D. Shakila said to the waiter you bring me a cup of coffee.

Q.5 Direction: Choose the option that is the direct form of the sentence.

My neighbour enquired how my father was.

A. My neighbour asked, "What about your father's welfare?"
B. My neighbour enquired, "How is your father?"
C. My neighbour asked, "How my father was?"
D. My neighbour enquired, "How is my father?"

Ques (6-7):Direction: Choose the option that is the direct form of the sentence.

Q.6 He exclaimed sadly that it was a pity that so many lives had been lost in the floods.

A. He said sadly, "It is a pity that so many lives had been lost in the floods."
B. He said sadly, "What a pity that so many lives are being lost in the floods!"
C. He said sadly, "What a pity that so many lives have been lost in the floods."
D. He said sadly, "It was a pity that so many lives were loss in the floods."

Q.7 The teacher asked the students if they had understood her question.

A. The teacher asked the students, "Have you understood her question?"
B. The teacher asking the students, "If you have understood my question?"
C. The teacher asked the students, "Have you understood my question?"
D. The teacher asks the students, "whether you understand my question?"

Q.8 Direction: Choose the option that is the indirect form of the sentence.

"I have joined computer classes" Rudra said.

A. Rudra said that he had joined computer classes.
B. Rudra said that I am joining computer classes.
C. Rudra said that I joined computer classes
D. Rudra said that I join computer classes.

Q.9 Direction: Choose the option that is the direct form of the sentence.

Vikas said to Navin that he hadn't met him since February the previous year.

A. Vikas told Navin, "You haven't meeting me since February last year."
B. Vikas said to Navin, "I haven't met you since February last year."
C. Vikas told to Navin, "I haven't met him since February last year."
D. Vikas said, "Navin, I haven't meet you since February last year."

Q.10 Direction: Choose the option that is the direct form of the sentence.

Devi replied that she was sorry but she could not go.

A. Devi replied, " She was sorry I could not go."
B. Devi replied, "Sorry she could not go."
C. Devi replied, "I'm sorry but I cannot go."
D. Devi replies, "I could not went but sorry."

Q.11 Direction: Choose the option that is the direct form of the sentence.

Abdul said that he had seen that film the day before.

A. Abdul said, "I had seen this film the day before."
B. Abdul said, "I saw this film yesterday."
C. Abdul said, "I saw that film yesterday."
D. Abdul said, "I see this film on the previous day."

Q.12 Direction: Choose the option that is the indirect form of the sentence.

Kishore said "I'm leaving now."
A. Kishore said that he was leaving then.
B. Kishore said that he left then.
C. Kishore says that I am leaving now.
D. Kishore said that he had to leaving then.

Ques (13-20):Direction: In the following question, a sentence has been given in Direct/Indirect Speech. Out of the four alternatives suggested, select the one which best expresses the same sentence in Indirect/Direct Speech.

Q.13 Tom said to me, "I shall meet you at the station".
A. Tom told me that he would meet me at the station.
B. Tom told me that he will meet me at the station.
C. Tom told me that I would meet me at the station.
D. Tom told me that he would have met me at the station.

Q.14 Ram says to me, "You are smart".
A. Ram tells me that I am smart.
B. Ram tells me that you are smart.
C. Ram tells me that I was smart.
D. Ram told me that I am smart.

Q.15 The boss said to her secretary, "Did you discuss this matter with the manager"?
A. The boss asked her secretary whether she discussed that matter with the manager.
B. The boss asked her secretary if you have discussed that matter with the manager.
C. The boss asked her secretary if she had discussed that matter with the manager.
D. The boss asked her secretary whether she has discussed that matter with the manager.

Q.16 The robber said to Alexander, "I am your captive".
A. The robber told Alexander that he is his captive.
B. The robber told Alexander that he was your captive.
C. The robber told to Alexander that he was his captive.
D. The robber told Alexander that he was his captive.

Q.17 The holy prophet said, "God helps those who help others".
A. The holy prophet said that God helped those who helped others.
B. The holy prophet said that God helps those who help others.
C. The holy prophet said that God helps people who help others.
D. The holy prophet said that God helps those people who help others.

Q.18 She asked her brother if he could give her some money then.
A. She said to her brother, "Could I give you some money now?"
B. She said to her brother, "Can you give me some money then?"
C. She said to her brother, "Can you give me some money now?"
D. She asked her brother, "Give me some money now."

Q.19 He said, "I will return tomorrow".
A. He said that he will return tomorrow.
B. He said that he would return tomorrow.
C. He said that he would return the next day.
D. He said that I would return the next day.

Q.20 'Why has the clock stopped?' thought Peter.
A. Peter wondered why the clock had stopped.
B. Peter wanted to know why the clock had stopped.
C. Peter asked why the clock had stopped.
D. Peter was thinking why the clock had stopped.

Q.21 Direction: Select the correct indirect form of the given sentence.

The landlord said to me, "Did you pay the water bill on time?"
A. The landlord asked me did I paid the water bill on time.
B. The landlord asked me if I had paid the water bill on time.
C. The landlord asked to me that did I pay the water bill on time.
D. The landlord asked me if I paid the water bill on time.

Q.22 Direction: Select the correct indirect form of the given sentence.

The tailor said to him, "Your shirt will be ready by tomorrow."
A. The tailor told him that his shirt will be ready by tomorrow.
B. The tailor told to him that your shirt will be ready by the next day.
C. The tailor told him that his shirt would be ready by the next day.
D. The tailor told him that your shirt would be ready by tomorrow.

Q.23 Direction: Select the correct direct form of the given sentence.

The doctor asked her what medicine she had taken then.
A. The doctor said to her, "What medicine have you taken now?"
B. The doctor said to her, "What medicine you are taking now?"
C. The doctor said to her, "What were medicine you have taken then?"
D. The doctor said to her, "What medicine you have taken then?"

Q.24 Direction: Select the correct direct form of the given sentence.

I told him that if he went around the park he would see some rare flowers.
A. I said to him, "If he went around the park he will see some rare flowers."
B. I said to him, "If you went around the park you would see some rare flowers."

C. I said to him, "If you go around the park you will see some rare flowers."

D. I said to him, "If you go around the park you would saw some rare flowers."

Q.25 Direction: Select the correct indirect form of the given sentence.

He exclaimed, "What a fine piece of architecture it is!"

A. He exclaimed was it a fine piece of architecture.
B. He exclaimed what a fine piece of architecture is it.
C. He exclaimed that what a fine piece of architecture it was.
D. He exclaimed that it was a fine piece of architecture.

Q.26 Direction: Select the correct indirect form of the given sentence.

Mahesh said to Priya, "How will you pay off your debts?"

A. Mahesh asked Priya how will she pay off her debts.
B. Mahesh asked Priya how she would pay off her debts.
C. Mahesh asked Priya how she would pay off your debts.
D. Mahesh asked Priya that how you will pay off your debts.

Q.27 Direction: Select the correct direct form of the given sentence.

Saaransh said that he had solved the crossword the previous day

A. Saaransh said, "He has solved the crossword the previous day."
B. Saaransh said, "I have solved the crossword the previous day."
C. Saaransh said, "He have solved the crossword yesterday."
D. Saaransh said, "I solved the crossword yesterday."

Q.28 Direction: Select the correct direct form of the given sentence.

I told my parents not to worry about me.

A. I said to my parents, "You don't be worried about me."
B. I said to my parents, "Don't worry about me."
C. I said to my parents, "You don't have to worry about me."
D. I said to my parents, "Nothing to worry about me."

Ques (29-30):Direction: Select the correct indirect form of the given sentence.

Q.29 Vandana said, "I'm being dropped to office today''.

A. Vandana said that she should be dropped to office today.
B. Vandana said that I am being dropped to office on that day.
C. Vandana said that she was being dropped to office that day.
D. Vandana said she was dropped to office today.

Q.30 "Do you attend the film festival at Goa every year?" he asked.

[SSC CHSL (Combined Higher Secondary Level), 2020]

A. He is asking me if I attended the film festival at Goa every year.
B. He had asked me if I was attending the film festival at Goa every year.
C. He asked me if I attend the film festival at Goa every year.
D. He asks me if I attend the film festival at Goa every year.

// Smart Answer Sheet //

Correct Indicates percentage of students who answered questions correctly.

Skipped Indicates percentage of students who skipped questions.

Q.	Ans.	Correct	Skipped
1	C	42.57 %	36.02 %
2	D	69.65 %	30.35 %
3	B	46.46 %	42.13 %
4	A	60.79 %	34.8 %
5	B	48.64 %	47.79 %
6	C	61.81 %	31.5 %
7	C	68.45 %	31.49 %
8	A	68.6 %	30.4 %
9	B	62.6 %	32.1 %
10	C	45.06 %	33.35 %
11	B	62.8 %	35.79 %
12	A	46.8 %	43.59 %
13	A	42.58 %	53.19 %
14	A	66.54 %	32.72 %
15	C	52.73 %	30.11 %
16	D	42.62 %	33.53 %
17	B	54.27 %	41.72 %
18	C	45.09 %	34.95 %
19	C	52.29 %	33.36 %
20	A	67.67 %	31.92 %
21	B	61.64 %	37.04 %
22	C	41.59 %	51.47 %
23	A	52.57 %	38.48 %
24	C	56.05 %	32.19 %
25	D	66.71 %	30.25 %
26	B	62.6 %	30.56 %
27	D	59.82 %	33.73 %
28	B	46.91 %	41.18 %
29	C	51.91 %	45.5 %
30	C	52.32 %	45.01 %

Performance Analysis	
Avg. Score (%)	50.0%
Toppers Score (%)	60.0%
Your Score	

//Hints and Solutions//

1. The correct answer is Lokesh said that he was very busy that week.

In the indirect form, first person changes to third person. So, 'I' will change to 'he'. We can reject options (A) and (B). 'He' is singular so it cannot be followed by 'are'. Option (D) is incorrect. The present tense form will be changed to past tense.

Hence, the correct option is (C).

2. The correct answer is:

Deepa told her friends that they were going to Tirupati the following week.

In the indirect form, the first person changes to the third person.

So, 'we' will change to 'they'.

Also, 'next week' changes to 'the following week'.

The given sentence is in present continuous form (are going).

Thus, it will change to past continuous form (were going).

The rest of the sentence remains the same.

Hence, the correct option is (D).

3. The correct answer is:

The Principal said to them, "I do not want to see any one to return with a complaint against you."

In the direct form, the second person changes to first person.

So, 'he' will change to 'I' as it is referring to the principal and 'them' will change to 'you' as it refers to the object i.e., them.

'Did' changes to 'do' in the direct form.

The sentence is in simple present tense so the direct form will also be in the simple present tense.

Hence, the correct option is (B).

4. The correct answer is:

Shakila told the waiter to bring her a cup of coffee.

Said is used when the speaker is making a statement and told is used when the speaker is giving an order.

So, here 'told' should be used. We are left with options (A) and (C).

The statement is in the simple present tense so the indirect form will be in the present tense.

Option (C) is grammatically incorrect as 'should' cannot be used with the past tense form of the verb.

Hence, the correct option is (A).

5. The correct answer is:

My neighbour enquired, "How is your father?"

Since the neighbor is enquiring, the direct form will be a question. The indirect form is in simple past tense as indicated by 'was'. So, the direct form will be in the simple present tense. 'Was' will be changed to 'is'. Also, the first person pronoun (my) will be changed to second person (your) in the direct form.

Hence, the correct option is (B).

6. The word 'exclaimed' states that the direct form will be an exclamation. The indirect form is in past perfect tense as indicated by the words 'had been'. So, the direct form will be in the present perfect tense.

Option (A) is in the past perfect tense.

Option (B) is in the present continuous tense.

Option (D) is grammatically incorrect as it uses 'loss' with 'were'.

Hence, the correct option is (C).

7. The correct answer is:

The teacher asked the students, "Have you understood my question?"

The given statement is in the past perfect tense as observed by the words 'had understood'. So, the direct form will be in present perfect tense i.e., it will contain 'have'. We can reject options (B) and (D).

In the sentence, 'her' refers to the speaker which is the teacher so in the direct form it will be changed to 'my'. Thus, option (A) can be eliminated as well.

Hence, the correct option is (C).

8. The correct answer is:

Rudra said that he had joined computer classes.

The given sentence is in present perfect tense as indicated by the words 'have joined'. So, the indirect form will be in past perfect tense. In indirect form, 'I' changes to second person pronoun. In this case it will be 'he'.

Option (B) is present continuous form.

Option (C) is in past tense.

Option (D) is in simple present tense.

Hence, the correct option is (A).

9. The correct answer is:

Vikas said to Navin, "I haven't met you since February last year."

The given sentence is in the indirect form. When we convert it to the direct mode of narration, we have to make the following changes:

The verb must change its form. Past perfect becomes present perfect.

'The previous year' becomes 'last year'.

The third person pronoun 'he' is changed into the second person pronoun 'you'.

'Him' is changed into the personal pronoun 'me'.

Hence, the correct option is (B).

10. The correct answer is:

Devi replied, "I'm sorry but I cannot go."

In the direct form, 'she' changes to 'I'. So, we are left with option (C) and (D). The given sentence is in simple past tense, which means the direct form will be in simple present tense. So, 'was' will be replaced by 'am' and 'could not' will be replaced with 'cannot'.

Hence, the correct option is (C).

11. The correct answer is:

Abdul said, "I saw this film yesterday."

In the direct form 'the day before' is changed to 'yesterday'. We are left with options (B) and (C). The indirect form is is past perfect tense which means the direct form will be in past tense. 'That' changes to 'this' in the direct form.

Hence, the correct option is (B).

12. The correct answer is:

Kishore said that he was leaving then.

The given statement is in the present continuous tense. So, the indirect form will be in the past continuous tense. In indirect form, 'now' changes to 'then'.

Option (B) is in the simple past tense.

Option (C) is in the present continuous tense.

Option (D) is grammatically incorrect.

Hence, the correct option is (A).

13. The given sentence is of direct speech. "Said to" will change to "told". Since the reporting verb is in the past tense, changes will be made to the reported verb. "Shall" will change to "would" as the pronoun "I" will change to "he". Option (A) follows the rules correctly, so, it is the correct answer.

Hence, the correct option is (A).

14. We know that if the reporting verb is in the present or future tense, no changes are made to the verb/tense of the reported speech.

For the given sentence, "says to" will change to "tells". "You" will change to "I". As we can see that option (A) follows the rules correctly, so it is the correct answer.

Hence, the correct option is (A).

15. The given sentence is in interrogative form. To convert such sentences into the indirect narration, the below rules are followed:

Say/Said is changed to ask/asked/wonder/wondered/enquire of/enquired of etc as per the sense of the sentence.

If the reported speech is in the form of WH-Question (who/what/why/how/where/when/which etc), no conjunction is used before the question word. The question word itself works as conjunction.

So, the correct answer will be:

The boss asked her secretary if she had discussed that matter with the manager.

Hence, the correct option is (C).

16. The given sentence is indirect speech. To convert it into indirect speech, we'll convert "said to" into "told". The tense of the reported speech is simple present which will change to simple past. The pronoun "I" is the first-person pronoun. First-person pronoun changes according to the subject of the reporting speech which is "robber" in the sentence. So, "I" will change to "he" in indirect speech. "Your" is a second-person pronoun. Second-person pronoun changes according to the object of the reporting verb which is Alexander in the sentence. So, "your" will change to "his". Option (D) follows these rules correctly, so it is the answer.

Hence, the correct option is (D).

17. The given sentence is in direct speech. Since the reporting verb "said" is not being followed by any object here, it will remain the same in indirect speech. Inverted commas will be replaced by the conjunction "that". The reported speech consists of a proverb and in this case, we do not change the tense of the reported speech. So, it will be written the same in indirect speech. Option (B) is the correct answer as it follows these rules.

Hence, the correct option is (B).

18. The given sentence is the direct speech of an interrogative sentence. So, "asked to" will change back to "said to". The conjunction "if" will be removed and the part ahead of it will be quoted in inverted commas. Since the modal verb here is "could" which is the past of "can", we'll use "can" to start the reported speech. "Her" will change to "me" and the word "then" will change to "now". Option (C) adheres to these rules, so it is the correct answer.

Hence, the correct option is (C).

19. The given sentence is in direct speech. The reporting verb "said" is not being followed by any object. So, "said" will not change to "told" and will remain the same. The verb "will" would change to its past form "would" and the word "tomorrow" will change to "the next day". The pronoun "I" is the first-person pronoun. First-person pronoun changes according to the subject of the reporting verb which is "he" here. Thus, "I" will change to "he". Option (C) adheres to these rules, so it is the correct answer.

Hence, the correct option is (C).

20. The given sentence is in interrogative form. Below are the steps to convert the sentence into indirect speech:

"thought" is an indication of wondering about something. So, it will change to "wondered".

The reported speech is in the form of WH-Question, so no conjunction is used before the question word. The question word itself works as a conjunction.

The reported verb is made assertive; i.e. it is kept in the order of subject + verb.

The tense of the reported speech will change from present perfect tense to past perfect tense.

Option (A) is the correct answer as it follows these rules.

Hence, the correct option is (A).

21. Indirect form- The landlord asked me if I had paid the water bill on time.

When the direct speech is in an interrogative form, we follow the steps given below:

- The reporting verb said to is converted into asked.
- The connector 'If' will follow the removal of comma and inverted commas.
- Change the reported speech from interrogative to assertive.
- Past simple tense (did you pay) in direct speech changes to past perfect in indirect speech (I had paid).

Hence, the correct option is (B).

22. Indirect form- The tailor told him that his shirt would be ready by the next day.

The basic rules for changing or converting direct speech into indirect speech:

- The commas and inverted commas are removed and 'that' is added.
- The second person 'your' will be changed into the first person 'his'.
- The future simple tense format 'Subject + will + V1 (be) + Object' will be changed into the present conditional tense format 'Subject + would + V1 (be) + Object'.

Hence, the correct option is (C).

23. Direct form- The doctor said to her, "What medicine have you taken now?"

The basic rules for changing or converting indirect speech into direct speech:

- The commas, inverted commas, and the question mark are added.
- The third person 'she' will be changed into the second person 'you'.
- The adverb "then" will become "now".
- The past perfect tense format 'Subject + had + V3 (taken) + Object' will be changed into the present perfect tense format 'Subject + have + V3 (taken) + Object'.

Hence, the correct option is (A).

24. Direct form- I said to him, "If you go around the park you will see some rare flowers."

The basic rules for changing or converting indirect speech into direct speech:

- The commas and inverted commas are added and 'that' is removed.
- The third person 'he' will be changed into the second person 'you'.
- The past simple tense format 'Subject + V2 (went) + Object' will be changed into the present simple tense format 'Subject + V1 (go) + Object'.
- The present conditional tense format 'Subject + would + V1 (see) + Object' will be changed into the future simple tense format 'Subject + will + V1 (see) + Object'.

Hence, the correct option is (C).

25. Indirect form- He exclaimed that it was a fine piece of architecture.

The basic rules for changing or converting direct speech into indirect speech:

- The commas, inverted commas and the questions mark are removed and 'that' is added.
- The full stop (.) is used in place of the exclamation mark (!).
- The present simple tense format 'Subject + V1 (is) + Object' will be changed into the past simple tense format 'Subject + V2 (was) + Object'.

Hence, the correct option is (D).

26. Indirect form- 'Mahesh asked Priya how she would pay off her debts.'

The basic rules for changing or converting direct speech into indirect speech:

- 'Said to' will be changed into 'asked' because the given sentence is an example of an interrogative sentence with a question word.
- Comma and inverted commas will be removed.
- 'How' will be used as a conjunction because we know that in an interrogative sentence with a question word the question word itself becomes the conjunction.
- 'Will' will be changed into 'would'. (Direct to Indirect form)
- 'You' will be changed into 'she'. (Second-person -> Third-person)
- 'Your' will be changed into 'her'. (Second-person -> Third-person)

Hence, the correct option is (B).

27. Direct form- Saaransh said, "I solved the crossword yesterday."

The basic rules for changing or converting indirect speech into direct speech:

- 'Said' will not change because in the given sentence reporting verb does not have any 'object'.
- Comma and inverted commas will be added.
- 'He' will be changed into 'I' because we know that it changes according to the subject of the reporting verb.
- Here, the subject of the reporting verb is "Sarransh".

- 'Had solved' will be changed into 'solved'. Because we know that the given sentence is in the past tense and V2 is changed into 'Had+V3' (past perfect tense changes to simple past tense).
- 'The previous day' will be changed into 'yesterday'. (indirect form to direct form)

Hence, the correct option is (D).

28. Direct form- I said to my parents, "Don't worry about me."

The basic rules for changing or converting indirect speech into direct speech:

- The given sentence is an example of an imperative sentence.
- Usually in an imperative sentence reporting verb is changed to 'ordered, advised, requested, commanded, beg, forbade, suggested, proposed, assured, asked, reminded, warned, agreed, refused, promised, etc.
- But in the given question reporting verb is 'Told'. So, we have to transform sentences accordingly.
- 'Told' will be changed into 'said to'.
- Comma and inverted commas will be added.
- We know that in imperative sentences 'not to/to' is added in indirect speech. So, in 'direct speech', 'not to' will be changed into 'Don't'.

Hence, the correct option is (B).

29. The correct sentence is: Vandana said that she was being dropped to office that day.

In the indirect form, 'today' changes to 'that day'. So, we can reject option (A) and (D).

The first person pronoun i.e., 'I' changes to third person i.e., 'she'.

The direct form is in present continuous form as indicated by (being dropped). So, the indirect form will be in past continuous form (was being dropped). Therefore, option (B) can also be rejected.

The only option which shows the structure of past continuous form is option (C).

Hence, the correct option is (C).

30. The correct sentence is:

He asked me if I attend the film festival at Goa every year.

- The question mark (?) is removed and a full stop (.) is used at the end of a sentence.
- The given example is an interrogative sentence starting with a helping verb, therefore, 'do' will be replaced with 'if/whether'.
- The second person 'you' will be changed into 'I'.
- The interrogative statement is changed into an assertive statement (helping verb will come after the subject).
- If reported speed in past/present routine action(here every year shows the routine action) then, there is no change in tense of reported speech.

Hence, the correct option is (C).

Q.1 Direction: Choose the correct answer to fill the blanks from the options given below:

After the driver ________ the car out of the bush, we climbed back into the car.

A. backs **B.** is backing
C. has backed **D.** had backed

Q.2 Direction: Choose the correct answer to fill the blanks from the options given below:

He won the match quite easily ________ he was out of practice.

A. even though **B.** in case
C. even if **D.** so that

Q.3 Direction: Choose the appropriate articles to complete the given sentence.

Mr. Mukesh went to market by____rickshaw to buy____book and returned by rickshaw.

A. a, a **B.** an, a
C. the, a **D.** no article, a

Q.4 Direction: Choose the appropriate articles to complete the given sentence.

Any change in ______ risk-o-meter reading with regard to ______ scheme shall be communicated to the unit-holders of that scheme said SEBI.

A. a, the **B.** the, a **C.** a, an **D.** an, a

Q.5 Direction: Choose the appropriate preposition to complete the given sentence.

"One should not be indifferent ________ the suffering of others."

A. about **B.** to **C.** of **D.** at

Q.6 Direction: Fill in the blank with the correct form of the tense.

Naina _______ watching movies for 3 hours when her mother came.

A. has been **B.** had been **C.** had **D.** is

Q.7 Direction: Fill in the blank with the correct form of the tense.

I _____ the food yet, so you have to wait for some time.

A. haven't cooked **B.** haven't cook
C. didn't cook **D.** hadn't cook

Q.8 Direction: Fill in the blank with the correct form of the tense.

I _______ studying for two hours before going to the exam hall tomorrow.

A. have been **B.** am
C. was **D.** will have been

Q.9 Direction: Fill the blanks in with the correct article.

______ lioness was very fierce but she could not save herself from _____ flood.

A. An, a **B.** A, a **C.** An, an **D.** The, the

Q.10 Direction: The following sentence in this section has a blank space and four words or groups of words are given after the sentence. Select the most appropriate word or group of words for the blank space and indicate your response accordingly.

Honesty is ______ on his face.

A. wrote **B.** written **C.** writing **D.** writes

Q.11 Direction: Select the appropriate word from the given options below to complete the sentence.

A person suffering from chronic neurodegenerative disease ______ short-term memory loss.

A. experienced **B.** has experienced
C. is experiencing **D.** experiences

Q.12 Direction: Fill in the blanks with the suitable preposition in the given sentence:

She is ignorant ____the latest developments _______ the field of computers.

A. of, at **B.** at, of **C.** at, in **D.** of, in

Q.13 Direction: Fill in the blank with the CORRECT conjunction in the given sentence:

They like the food in that restaurant, ______ they go there very often.

A. because **B.** therefore **C.** since **D.** if

Q.14 Direction: Choose the most suitable answer to fill the blank:

If you had told me you needed a ride, I _____ earlier.

A. would have left
B. would have been left
C. will have left
D. will be leaving

Q.15 Direction: Choose the correct answer to fill the blanks from the options given below:

Annu, though ill-equipped for the project, had ______ tried her best.

A. for **B.** nevertheless
C. last **D.** if

Q.16 Direction: Choose the correct answer to fill the blanks from the options given below:

The ancient fountain was hidden ______ the trees.

A. among **B.** form **C.** follow **D.** during

Q.17 Direction: Choose the correct answer to fill the blanks from the options given below:

______ had she stepped out of her house when the rain started.

A. Scarce **B.** When
C. No sooner **D.** Hardly

Q.18 Direction: Choose the correct answer to fill the blanks from the options given below:

Interest to serve the merchants has been ______ since digitization ______ at the merchant's end.

A. grown, started **B.** growing, started
C. grow, started **D.** growing, starting

Q.19 Direction: Choose the correct answer to fill the blanks from the options given below:

Unemployment rate ______ in the US as govt stimulus for recovery ______.

A. rises, fades **B.** rise, faded
C. rose, fading **D.** rises, faded

Q.20 Direction: Choose the correct answer to fill the blanks from the options given below:

As the ATM ran out of _____ , the manager ordered to get money from the _____ to refill the ATM.

A. cash, cash **B.** cash, cache
C. cache, cache **D.** cache, cash

Q.21 Direction: Choose the correct answer to fill the blanks from the options given below:

Presidential ______ (assent / ascent) is a must ______ (in /on /for) the new Legislation.

A. assent, in **B.** ascent, on
C. assent, for **D.** ascent, in

Q.22 Direction: Choose the correct answer to fill the blanks from the options given below:

If you wish to survive here, you must prove your _____.

You ought ______ to touch the fire unless you want to get burned.

A. medal, knot **B.** mettle, not
C. meddle, nought **D.** metal, note

Q.23 Direction: Choose the correct answer to fill the blanks from the options given below:

Galileo _____ that the Earth _____ around the Sun.

A. discovers, moved
B. discovered, had moved
C. discovered, moves
D. discovers, has moved

Q.24 Direction: Choose the correct answer to fill the blanks from the options given below:

Madhav left in _____ hurry after eating ____ bowl of porridge, and _____ orange.

A. a, a, a **B.** the, a, a
C. the, the, a **D.** a, a, an

Q.25 Direction: Choose the correct answer to fill the blanks from the options given below:

a. What's your skirt made from? It ____ like wool.

b. I won't be coming to work today. I _____ very well. (feel)

A. feels, not feeling **B.** feels, don't feel
C. is feeling, feeling **D.** is feeling, feeling

Q.26 Direction: Choose the correct answer to fill the blanks from the options given below:

The ________ of our civilization from an agricultural society to today's complex industrial world was accompanied by war.

A. Adjustment **B.** Migration
C. Route **D.** Metamorphosis

Q.27 Direction: Choose the correct answer to fill the blanks from the options given below:

The defendant is accused of attempting to ______ evidence.

A. expose **B.** verdict **C.** conceal **D.** bare

Q.28 Direction: Choose the correct answer to fill the blanks from the options given below:

The ________ of a tragedy usually brings death or ruin to the leading character.

A. salvation **B.** catastrophe
C. conservation **D.** saving

Q.29 Direction: Choose the correct answer to fill the blanks from the options given below:

The teenage boy began clenching his fists when he heard the _____ being rude to his friends

A. gentle **B.** bully **C.** mild **D.** patient

Q.30 Direction: Choose the correct answer to fill the blanks from the options given below:

The man who stole from the poor was a ______ thief.

A. compassionate **B.** concern
C. pity **D.** callous

// Smart Answer Sheet //

Correct Indicates percentage of students who answered questions correctly.

Skipped Indicates percentage of students who skipped questions.

Q.	Ans.	Correct	Skipped
1	D	58.44 %	40.59 %
2	A	49.75 %	37.14 %
3	D	42.75 %	51.97 %
4	B	56.58 %	41.53 %
5	B	46.58 %	53.15 %
6	B	68.46 %	30.32 %
7	A	40.02 %	58.19 %
8	D	43.77 %	37.98 %
9	D	50.72 %	32.03 %
10	B	65.06 %	32.68 %
11	D	44.6 %	50.25 %
12	D	63.58 %	31.21 %
13	B	44.05 %	42.64 %
14	A	63.05 %	31.84 %
15	B	61.57 %	30.46 %
16	A	66.25 %	30.1 %
17	D	53.62 %	42.98 %
18	B	49.18 %	34.87 %
19	A	40.27 %	50.31 %
20	B	42.91 %	45.07 %
21	C	54.64 %	30.33 %
22	B	49.85 %	30.81 %
23	C	54.41 %	38.15 %
24	D	59.22 %	33.9 %
25	B	55.53 %	30.76 %
26	D	59.26 %	33.68 %
27	C	43.34 %	36.71 %
28	B	61.29 %	32.53 %
29	B	53.3 %	31.33 %
30	D	67.44 %	32.35 %

Performance Analysis	
Avg. Score (%)	36.67%
Toppers Score (%)	63.33%
Your Score	

//Hints and Solutions//

1. The complete sentence is: After the driver **had backed** the car out of the bush, we climbed back into the car.

The second verb of the sentence is 'climbed', which shows simple past tense. The action shown by the first sentence happens 'before' the action of the second sentence, viz, we climbed back into the car. This means that the verb in the blank is showing an action happening even before the action shown by simple past tense verb 'climbed'. So, we must use past perfect tense in such cases. The past perfect tense form is only reflected by the verb 'had backed'.

Hence, the correct option is (D).

2. The correct sentence is: "He won the match quite easily **even though** he was out of practice."

The blank divides two complete sentences. So the blank must contain conjunction

The first sentence is 'He won the match quite easily', while the second says that 'he was out of practice'. The second sentence is negative in meaning, in the sense that, it is not supporting the first sentence.

This means that the first action happened 'in spite of' the second action OR 'He won the match easily despite the fact that he was out of practice'. So, the conjunction in the blank must mean 'in spite of' or 'despite'.

Thus, the only option that reflects this meaning is 'even though'.

Hence, the correct option is (A).

3. The correct sentence is: "Mr. Mukesh went to market **by rickshaw** to buy **a** book and returned by rickshaw."

The most appropriate articles to complete the given sentence is 'no article, a'.

In the first blank, no article should be used with the means of transportation which are preceded by the preposition 'by'.

For example:

- Mohit will go to Rajasthan **by the bus** but will return in a cab. (Wrong)
- Mohit will go to Rajasthan **by bus** but will return in a cab. (Correct)

In the second blank, the most appropriate article is 'a' because 'book' has a consonant sound. And we use the article 'a' before a consonant sound.

- For example: a car, a house, a big truck, a wheel, a grey day, etc.

Hence, the correct option is (D).

4. The correct sentence is: Any change in **the** risk-o-meter reading with regard to **a** scheme shall be communicated to the unit-holders of that scheme said SEBI.

The most appropriate articles in the given fill in the blanks are 'the, a'.

In the first blank, the most appropriate article is 'The' because the article 'The' before a noun shows that what is referred to is already known to the speaker, listener, writer, and/or reader (it is the definite article).

- For example: We had to paint **the** apartment before we sold it. (The speaker and the listener know what apartment is being referred to.)

Here, in the given question 'risk-o-meter' is a specific noun. Therefore, the definite article 'the' should be used here.

In the second blank, the most appropriate article is 'a' because 'scheme' has a consonant sound. The given question is talking about all the schemes in general. Therefore, the most appropriate article is 'a'.

Hence, the correct option is (B).

5. The correct sentence is, "One should not be indifferent **to** the suffering of others."

In the given sentence, the word indifferent is used. Indifferent means marked by a lack of interest, enthusiasm, or concern for something. The prepositions used with indifferent are to, toward or towards. The preposition 'to' is used for a motive/reason.

- For example: The children arrived at the park **to** meet their friends.

Hence, the correct option is (B).

6. The complete sentence is, "Naina **had been** watching movies for 3 hours when her mother came."

The past perfect continuous tense is used to say that an action begun before a certain point of time in the past and continued up to that time.

- For example: He **had been** sleeping for 2 hours when the alarm rang.

The general structure of past perfect continuous tense is- had+ been + V1+ ing.

Hence, the correct option is (B).

7. The complete sentence is,"I **haven't cooked** the food yet, so you have to wait."

The presence of yet at the end of the sentence indicates that present perfect tense should be used in the sentence.

Yet is used as an adverb to refer to a time that starts in the past and continues up to the present. We use it mostly in negative statements or questions in the present perfect. It usually comes in the end position.

Present perfect tense combines the present tense and the perfect aspect used to express an event that happened in the past that has present consequences. The structure of the present perfect tense is as follows:

- Subject + has/have + past participle (V3) + object.

For example:

- **Has** she emailed you yet?
- I **haven't** talked to her yet.

Hence, the correct option is (A).

8. The correct sentence is, "I **will have been** studying for two hours before going to the exam hall tomorrow."

As the sentence here refers to the future and the time expression 'for two hours' has been used which suggests that the most appropriate tense to be used here is future perfect continuous tense.

The syntax for the future perfect continuous tense-

- Sub+ will have been/shall have been+ ing form of verb.

For example: In November, I **will have been** working at my company for three years.

Hence, the correct option is (D).

9. The correct sentence is 'The lioness was very fierce but she could not save herself from the flood'.

In the given sentence, 'The' is used in the first blank, and 'the' is used in the second blank.

According to grammar, 'Use the definite article 'the' when the noun is known to the reader, is previously mentioned in the speech or is specific to the situation'.

Let's see some examples:

- The giraffe had a short neck which is why all the other giraffes made fun of him.
- The earthquake that hit Miami was the biggest one yet.

In the first blank, 'lioness' refers to a very specific lioness who was fierce, not all lionesses are fierce and not all of them are unable to save themselves from floods. In the second blank, 'flood' refers to a very specific flood from which the lioness in question could not save herself.

Hence, the correct option is (D).

10. The correct sentence is: Honesty is written on his face.

In the given options the correct verb to fill in the blank is 'written.'

As we can understand that the sentence is in the passive voice. And the structure of passive voice for the present indefinite tense is:

Structure: Subject + is/am/are + verb (3rd form) + object.

- Example: The gate is opened by the peon.

So, we should add 3rd form of the verb (written) after the helping verb (is).

Hence, the correct option is (B).

11. Complete sentence: A person suffering from chronic neurodegenerative disease experiences short-term memory loss.

The given sentence is giving a general information about what happens to a person diagnosed with neurodegenerative disease.

Present Indefinite Tense represents an action which is regular or normal or true and uses the base form of the verb. In case of the third person singular number, 's or es' is added with the verb.

- Example: We watch movies in this Cineplex.

Among the given options, 'experiences' is the verb form of present indefinite tense.

Hence, the correct option is (D).

12. Correct Sentence: She is ignorant of the latest developments in the field of computers.

The most appropriate preposition in the given sentence is 'of, in'.

In the first filler, 'of' should be used because 'ignorant of something' is a phrasal verb.

It means 'not knowing about something.'

- Example: Many people are ignorant of their rights.

In the second filler, 'in' should be used because it means inside a container, place, or area, or surrounded or closed off by something.

- Example: This led to the development of tourism in Goa.

Hence, the correct option is (D).

13. The correct sentence is: They like the food in that restaurant, therefore they go there very often.

'Therefore' means for that reason; consequently.

- Example: He was injured and therefore unable to play.

In the given sentence they like the food of a restaurant as a result of which they go there very often.

Therefore, the most appropriate conjunction in the given blank is 'therefore'.

Hence, the correct option is (B).

14. Correct sentence: If you had told me you needed a ride, I would have left earlier.

The given sentence is the type 3 conditional.

The type 3 conditional is used to refer to a time that is in the past, and a situation that is contrary to reality.

The structure of type 3 conditional is:

- If clause: If + past perfect
- Main clause: perfect conditional or perfect continuous conditional
- Example: If it had rained you would have gotten wet.

Hence, the correct option is (A).

15. The most appropriate word to fill in the given blank is 'nevertheless'.

- The word 'nevertheless' means 'in spite of that
  - Example: It was a cold, rainy day. Nevertheless, more people came than we had expected.
- We use 'nevertheless' when saying something that contrasts with what has just been said.

Hence, the correct option is (B).

16. The most appropriate word to fill in the given blank is 'among'.

- The word 'among' means 'surrounded by; in the middle.
  - Example: I often feel nervous when I'm among strangers.
- Among is used when someone or something that is situated or moving among a group of things or people is surrounded by them.

Hence, the correct option is (A).

17. The correct answer is 'Hardly'.

- 'Hardly.... when' is correlative conjunction; we use hardly at the beginning of a sentence before an auxiliary to say that one thing happens very soon after another thing
- 'Hardly' is always used with 'when' whereas 'No sooner' is used with 'than'.
- For e.g: Hardly had the bell rung when he started running out of his classroom
- So, according to the above-mentioned points 'hardly' is the correct answer.

Other options are rejected because:

- 'Scarce' is an adjective that means 'hard to find, not often found.
- 'When' and 'as soon as' are grammatically incorrect for the sentence.

Hence, the correct option is (D).

18. The correct answer is growing, started.

The second option is correct as 'growing' is the present participle of the verb, the present perfect continuous is formed using has/have + been + present participle and 'started' is the past tense of the verb.

The first option is incorrect as 'grown' is the past participle form of the verb. 'Started' is still okay for the second blank but 'grown' is not fit for the first blank.

The third option is incorrect as 'grow' is the base or simple form of the verb. 'Started' is still okay for the second blank but 'grow' is not fit for the first blank.

The fourth option is incorrect as 'starting' is the present participle of the verb. 'Growing' is still okay for the first blank but 'starting' is not fit for the second blank.

Hence, the correct option is (B).

19. The correct answer is: Unemployment rate <u>rises</u> in the US as govt stimulus for recovery <u>fades</u>.

The first option is correct as the tense (simple present tense) of both the words are correct and also their meaning fits into the sentence. Also, the plural subject "unemployment rate" takes the plural verb 'rises'.

Hence, the correct option is (A).

20. Complete sentence: As the ATM ran out of <u>cash</u>, the manager ordered to get money from the <u>cache</u> to refill the ATM.

For the first blank, we need a word whose meaning is close to the money.

For the second blank, we need a word whose meaning is close to the hidden store.

Cash: money in the form of coins or notes and not cheques, plastic cards, etc.

Cache: a hidden store of things, or the place where they are kept.

After examining all the options, the correct pair is 'cash, cache.'

Hence, the correct option is (B).

21. Correct Sentence: Presidential <u>assent</u> is a must <u>for</u> the new Legislation.

For the first blank, we need a word whose meaning is close to an agreement.

- Assent: official agreement to something.

Therefore, the correct word for the first blank is assent.

- For: We use for to talk about a purpose or a reason for something.

Therefore, the correct preposition for the second blank is for.

Hence, the correct option is (C).

22. Complete sentence:

- If you wish to survive here, you must prove your <u>mettle</u>.
- You ought <u>not</u> to touch the fire unless you want to get burned.

Mettle: a person's ability to cope well with difficulties; spirit and resilience.

For the second blank, we need an adverb not because of the presence of the verb ought.

Hence, the correct option is (B).

23. Correct sentence: Galileo <u>discovered</u> that the Earth <u>moves</u> around the Sun.

The first part of the sentence must be in the Past Tense as it is talking about the discovery of Galileo which happened in the past.

- Therefore, the verb discovered is the correct choice for the first blank.

The second part of the sentence is a universal truth.

Therefore, it should be in the Present Tense.

- So, the verb moves is the correct choice for the second blank.

Hence, the correct option is (C).

24. Madhav left in a hurry after eating a bowl of porridge, and an orange.

'A' is used with a singular countable noun that is random in nature and has a consonant sound.

'An' is used with a singular countable noun that is random in nature and has a vowel sound.

'The' refers to a particular object of which the reader is aware of.

- The words 'hurry' and 'bowl' start with a consonant, therefore an article 'a' is used.
- The word 'orange' starts with a vowel, therefore, an article 'an' is used.

Therefore, the word 'a, a, an' should be used.

Hence, the correct option is (D).

25. Correct sentence:

a. What's your skirt made from? It feels like wool.

b. I won't be coming to work today. I don't feel very well.

We commonly use the pronoun it as both a subject and an object pronoun.

It always takes a singular verb.

- Example: It is too expensive for us.

I is a singular pronoun but it always takes a plural verb.

- Example: I don't want to go there.

Hence, the correct option is (B).

26. The <u>metamorphosis</u> of our civilization from an agricultural society to today's complex industrial world was accompanied by war.

Metamorphosis: a complete change of form (as part of natural development)

The sentence implies here the transformation /changes in civilization (human society) from agriculture to today's industrial world were accompanied by war.

Hence, the correct option is (D).

27. From the sentence, we get to know that the defendant(an individual, company, or institution sued or accused in a court of law) might have tried to hide the evidence so he was accused of it.

In option (C), the word conceal means not allowed to be seen; hide.

Therefore, conceal is the only word that fits here appropriately.

So, the correct sentence is:

The defendant is accused of attempting to <u>conceal</u> evidence.

Hence, the correct option is (C).

28. From the sentence, we get to know that a tragic event usually brings sudden death or ruin to the leading character.

In option (B), the word catastrophe means an event causing great and usually sudden damage or suffering; a disaster.

Therefore, catastrophe is the only word that fits here appropriately.

So, the correct sentence is,

The catastrophe of a tragedy usually brings death or ruin to the leading character.

Hence, the correct option is (B).

29. From the sentence, we get to know that the teenage boy clenched his fists when some people were being rude to his friends.

In option (B), the word bully means a person who habitually seeks to harm or intimidate those whom they perceive as vulnerable.

Therefore, the bully is the only word that fits here appropriately.

So, the correct sentence is,

The teenage boy began clenching his fists when he heard the bully being rude to his friends

Hence, the correct option is (B).

30. From the sentence, we get to know that the thief must have had no emotions that he stole from a man who's already poor.

In option (D), the word callous means feeling no emotion or showing no sympathy for others.

Therefore, callous is the only word that fits here appropriately.

So, the correct sentence is:

The man who stole from the poor was a callous thief.

Hence, the correct option is (D).

Q.1 Direction: Choose the correct meaning of a given proverb/idiom.

Hit the nail on the head

[Allahabad High Court ARO, 2020]

A. Go to bed
B. Do or say something exactly right
C. Series of problems
D. Someone who lacks intelligence

Q.2 Direction: Chosen the correct option to complete the idiom which means "to overcome a barrier, especially the ones related to gender or race":

"To _____ through the glass ceiling"

[Allahabad High Court Review Officer (RO), 2019]

A. crack **B.** break **C.** beat **D.** melt

Q.3 Direction: Choose the correct meaning of the given idiom:

"Raining cats and dogs"

[Allahabad High Court Review Officer (RO), 2019]

A. very heavy rain
B. A strange event
C. A false gossip
D. Something impossible

Q.4 Direction: Choose the correct meaning of the given idiom:

"To tie the knot"

[Allahabad High Court Review Officer (RO), 2019]

A. Get married
B. Playing with a coir rope
C. Give a death penalty
D. Commit suicide

Q.5 Direction: Which of the given options best describes the meaning of the phrase.

"To stew in one's own juice"?

A. To eat healthy food
B. To suffer the results of one's own actions
C. To eat unhealthy food
D. To suffer the results of other's actions

Q.6 Direction: Select the most appropriate meaning of the underlined idiom in the given sentence.

Pradeep was so tired that he <u>hit the sack</u> as soon as possible.

A. Left work **B.** Went to bed
C. Accepted defeat **D.** Kicked the sack

Q.7 Direction: Select the most appropriate meaning of the underlined idiom in the given sentence.

My aunt has <u>the gift of the gab</u> and can socialize in any group.

A. ability to cook well
B. ability to criticize anyone
C. ability to spend time anywhere
D. ability to speak eloquently

Q.8 Select the most appropriate meaning of the underlined idiom in the given sentence.

The sad part of the agitation is that most of the leaders are only <u>paying lip-service</u> to the issue.

[SSC Sub Inspector (CPO), 2019]

A. Saying they agree although they do not support it
B. Partially impressing the crowds
C. Making long speeches for the cause
D. Growing angry and restless with the organizers

Ques (9-12):Direction: Choose the option which best expresses the meaning of the idiom/phrase given below.

Q.9 "Let the grass grow under one's feet"

[SSC Sub Inspector (CPO), 2018], [SSC Sub Inspector (CPO), 2017]

A. To accept responsibility
B. To engage in a project
C. To remain idle
D. To grow grass at home

Q.10 "Be in the same boat"

[SSC Sub Inspector (CPO), 2018], [SSC Sub Inspector (CPO), 2017]

A. To ask someone to travel on the same boat
B. To be in the same difficult situation
C. Willing to do something immediately
D. To force an issue that has already ended

Q.11 "High on the hog"

[SSC Sub Inspector (CPO), 2018], [SSC Sub Inspector (CPO), 2017]

A. To go to bed or go to sleep
B. To study for a test
C. To live in a luxurious or costly way
D. To have something secured

Q.12 "Cut to the chase"

[SSC Sub Inspector (CPO), 2018], [SSC Sub Inspector (CPO), 2017]

A. To start talking about the important aspects of something
B. To conclude from obvious fact
C. To clean solid lines
D. To be evil tempered

Q.13 Direction: In the following question, out of the four alternatives, select the alternative which best expresses the meaning of the idiom/phrase.

Nail colours to the mast

A. Put up a colourful mast
B. Refused to climb down
C. Took over the ship
D. Decided to abandon the ship

Q.14 Direction: In the following question, out of the four alternatives, choose the alternative which best expresses the meaning of the given idiom.

Apple Pie Order

A. In random order
B. Related to fruits packing
C. Related to dry fruit packing
D. In perfect order

Q.15 Direction: Select the most appropriate meaning of the underlined idiom in the given sentence.

Her success as a singer was a nine days' wonder.

[SSC CGL, 2020]

A. Eternal fame
B. A short-lived sensation
C. A proud achievement
D. An impossible feat

Q.16 Direction: Select the most appropriate meaning of the underlined idiom in the given sentence.

Information technology has developed by leaps and bounds.

A. very gradually
B. at a rapid pace
C. in far off places
D. through unfair means

Q.17 Direction: Choose the correct alternative which appropriately describes the given idioms and phrases.

Go to dogs

A. To go mad
B. To be insulted
C. To be ruined
D. To go brutal

Q.18 Direction: Some proverb/idiom is given below together with their meanings. Choose the correct meaning of proverb/idiom.

To cry wolf

A. To listen eagerly
B. To give false alarm
C. To turn pale
D. To keep off starvation

Q.19 Direction: Select the option that means the same as the given idiom.

To pull oneself together

A. To hide important facts and reasons
B. To put necessary matters on the table
C. To keep working constantly with attention
D. To calm oneself and begin to think or act

Q.20 Direction: Select the most appropriate meaning of the underlined idiom in the given sentence.

I will not go to work today as I am feeling under the weather.

A. Bad weather
B. Too hot to go out
C. Being sick
D. Rainy weather

Q.21 Direction: Select the best alternative that has the closest meaning to the underlined phrase.

Readers are advised to take this information with a grain of salt.

A. Taking something under consideration.
B. Taking responsibility to maintain privacy.
C. Not taking something too seriously.
D. Not taking something easily.

Q.22 Direction: Choose the option which best expresses the meaning of the idiom/phrase given below.

Be in the same boat

A. To ask someone to travel on the same boat
B. To be in the same difficult situation
C. Willing to do something immediately
D. To force an issue that has already ended

Q.23 Direction: Choose the option which gives the meaning of the phrase most appropriately in the context of the given sentence.

They go to the beach when they should be hitting the books and then they wonder why they get low marks.

A. Scrutinizing
B. Studying
C. Reflecting
D. Exploring

Ques (24-30):Direction: Choose the correct meaning of the idiom and mark the answer.

Q.24 Be in eclipse

A. Less successful
B. Feeling happy
C. Very successful
D. Being defeated

Q.25 Ways and means

A. A technique
B. Methods of achieving something
C. Norms and regulations of doing something
D. Improving one's way of doing

Q.26 Up in arms

A. Very happy
B. Very satisfied
C. Very angry
D. Feeling fine

Q.27 Bolt from the blue

A. An event or piece of news which is unexpected
B. Desirable event or news
C. An event which takes place as planned
D. News which has been long expected, but arrives late

Q.28 Spiff up

A. To make oneself look neat
B. To make oneself look untidy
C. To make oneself look arrogant
D. To appear on the stage as a baboon

Q.29 Mellow out

A. To feel bad about other's enjoyment
B. To like and dislike people concurrently
C. To enjoy oneself without doing much
D. To work hard and doing much work

Q.30 Jump on the bandwagon

A. To get out of difficulty
B. To judge by appearance
C. To join a popular trend

D. To get into trouble

// Smart Answer Sheet //

Correct Indicates percentage of students who answered questions correctly.

Skipped Indicates percentage of students who skipped questions.

Q.	Ans.	Correct	Skipped
1	B	51.14 %	34.92 %
2	B	40.48 %	49.18 %
3	A	50.75 %	42.45 %
4	A	46.18 %	50.85 %
5	B	44.51 %	41.1 %
6	B	63.01 %	31.04 %
7	D	52.96 %	30.85 %
8	A	58.33 %	33.13 %
9	C	60.72 %	37.25 %
10	B	40.17 %	50.44 %
11	C	66.84 %	32.94 %
12	A	48.57 %	35.01 %
13	B	69.59 %	30.02 %
14	D	51.26 %	45.75 %
15	B	54.13 %	34.15 %
16	B	69.04 %	30.03 %
17	C	68.9 %	30.17 %
18	B	61.48 %	37.65 %
19	D	58.4 %	34.91 %
20	C	59.43 %	39.96 %
21	C	68.32 %	30.31 %
22	B	64.54 %	30.58 %
23	B	46.32 %	31.81 %
24	A	64.29 %	35.14 %
25	B	63.39 %	34.64 %
26	C	67.31 %	31.64 %
27	A	51.58 %	31.75 %
28	A	63.2 %	31.3 %
29	C	59.86 %	36.95 %
30	C	69.64 %	30.18 %

Performance Analysis	
Avg. Score (%)	33.33%
Toppers Score (%)	70.0%
Your Score	

//Hints and Solutions//

1. Hit the nail on the head means to do or say something exactly right.

It means to do exactly the right thing; to do something in the most effective and efficient way.

Example: Every word he said hit the nail on the head.

Hence, the correct option is (B).

2. Correct answer: To **break** through the glass ceiling.

The meaning of the idiom 'to break through the glass ceiling' is to overcome invisible barriers that are related to gender or race.

For example: We need **to break through the glass ceiling** to survive in this organization.

Hence, the correct option is (B).

3. Raining cats and dogs: very heavily raining.

The English-language idiom "raining cats and dogs" is used to describe particularly heavy rain.

For example:

- It's raining cats and dogs I am worried about how my kids will reach home.
- It rains cats and dogs when the Monsoon comes to India.

From the above lines, we can say that Very heavy rain is the correct meaning of the given idiom.

Hence, the correct option is (A).

4. To tie the knot means to get married.

It also means to perform a marriage ceremony.

For example:

- So when are you two going to tie the knot?
- Christina and Bill are about to tie the knot. The wedding is on Saturday!

From the above lines, we can say that Get married is the correct meaning of the given idiom.

Hence, the correct option is (A).

5. To stew in one's own juice: Be left to suffer the consequences of one's own actions.

For example:

- Let him stew in his own juices for a while.
- He's run into debt again, but this time we're leaving him to stew in his own juice.

From the above lines, we can say that To suffer the results of one's own actions is the correct meaning of the given phrase.

Hence, the correct option is (B).

6. To Hit the sack means to go to bed.

Example: After the long journey, he hit the sack as soon as he reached home.

He wanted to hit the sack and did not feel like going out to party with his friends.

Hence, the correct option is (B).

7. 'Gift of the gab' is an idiom which means the ability to speak fluently and eloquently. A person with this gift would be a good orator.

Hence, the correct option is (D).

8. Let's look at the meaning of the given idiom:

Paying lip service - to say that you agree with something but do nothing to support it. For Example: The boss was merely paying lip service as he never committed to the idea.

Hence, the correct option is (A).

9. The meaning of the given idiom 'Let the grass grow under one's feet' is 'To be inactive; to do nothing or stand still.'

- Examples,
  - I used to let the grass grow under my feet, and I missed out on a lot of opportunities.
  - Mary doesn't let the grass grow under her feet. She's always busy.
- The word 'idle' means 'unemployed or unoccupied; inactive'.
- Therefore, from the given explanation and examples, option (C) is the correct answer.

Hence, the correct option is (C).

10. The meaning of the given idiom 'Be in the same boat' is 'be in the same unfortunate or unpleasant situation as others'.

- Examples,
  - My sister failed her driver's test, and I'll be in the same boat if I don't practice parallel parking.
  - None of us could pass the maths exam, so we're all in the same boat.
- From the explanation and examples that are given above, option (B) is the correct answer.

Hence, the correct option is (B).

11. The meaning of the given idiom 'High on the hog' is 'to live in great comfort with a lot of money'.

- Examples,
  - They've been living high on the hog ever since David won the lottery.
  - We aren't as wealthy as the Jones' to live so high on the hog.
- Therefore, according to the explanation and examples that are given above, option (C) is the correct answer.

Hence, the correct option is (C).

12. The meaning of the given idiom 'cut to the chase' is 'to start talking about the important aspects of something'

'To start talking about the important aspects of something' means to avoid talking about unnecessary things and focus on what is important.

- **Examples,**
  - I'm a very busy woman, so I need an assistant who can cut to the chase.
  - After a few introductory comments, we cut to the chase and began negotiating.

Hence, the correct option is (A).

13. Nail colours to the mast means to show one's intention to hold on to those beliefs until the end.

Hence, the correct option is (B).

14. Apple Pie Order means in perfect order. The meaning suggests that everything is arranged neatly, in the correct order, and perfectly in place. Also, that everything is sterile or to the highest level of cleanliness.

For example: On the eve of inspection every thing was kept in apple pie order.

Hence, the correct option is (D).

15. A nine days' wonder (idiom) - something that attracts great interest for a short while but is then forgotten.

Example: The song was a nine days' wonder.

Hence, the correct option is (B).

16. The correct answer is- at a rapid pace.

Given Idiom: By leaps and bounds means rapidly or in fast progress.

Example - Her French is improving by leaps and bounds

Hence, the correct option is (B).

17. Let's look at the meaning of the given idiom:

Go to the dogs- to become ruined or a much worse condition

Example: Our favorite restaurant has gone to the dogs lately.

Hence, the correct option is (C).

18. To cry wolf means to give false alarm. It means to keep asking for help when you do not need it, with the result that people think you do not need help when you really need it.

Example- "Don't pay attention to Peter, he's only crying wolf."

Hence, the correct option is (B).

19. To pull oneself together means to calm oneself and begin to think or act.

The phrase 'Pull onself together' means to get control of your emotions and actions.

Example: "He's finding it hard to pull himself together after the accident."

Hence, the correct option is (D).

20. The idiom 'under the weather' means 'slightly unwell or in low spirits.'

Therefore, 'being sick' is the correct answer.

Example- I don't feel like hanging out today. I'm feeling a bit under the weather.

Hence, the correct option is (C).

21. The meaning of the phrase "take with a grain of salt" means not taking something too seriously.

Example: The Indian players took the issue of racism with a grain of salt.

Hence, the correct option is (C).

22. The meaning of the idiom -"Be in the same boat" is 'To be in the same difficult situation'.

Example: When he lost his job he did not feel too bad as, after the company downsized, many others were in the same boat.

Hence, the correct option is (B).

23. "Hitting the books" means to study especially in time of tests and exams. Here the sentence means implying the meaning of the idiom as "They go to the beach when they should be studying really hard and then they wonder why they don't get good marks."

Hence, the correct option is (B).

24. The correct answer is Less successful.

Be in eclipse: much less successful and important than before

For example: Even when her career was temporarily in eclipse she had no financial worries.

Hence, the correct option is (A).

25. The correct answer is 'Methods of achieving something.'

Ways and means: The methods by which something is accomplished or attained, especially in relation to finances

For example: We're here to discuss the goals of the project, not the ways and means.

Hence, the correct option is (B).

26. The correct answer is 'Very angry.'

Up in arms: angry or rebellious

For example: My mom was up in arms about the new salary cuts rumored to be put in place.

Hence, the correct option is (C).

27. The correct answer is, 'An event or piece of news which is unexpected'.

Bolt from the blue: A sudden, unexpected event

For example: The resignation of the chairman came like a bolt from the blue.

Hence, the correct option is (A).

28. The correct answer is, 'To make oneself look neat'.

Spiff up: improve in appearance often by making more neat or stylish

For example: High-school students used to spiff up their college applications with extracurriculars like Model U.N. and student council.

Hence, the correct option is (A).

29. The correct answer is, 'To enjoy oneself without doing much'.

Mellow out: to become relaxed and calm

For example: My dad has definitely mellowed out as he's gotten older.

Hence, the correct option is (C).

30. The most appropriate meaning of the given idiom 'Jump on the bandwagon' means 'To join a popular trend'.

Jump on the bandwagon: join others in doing or supporting something fashionable or likely to be successful.

To join a popular trend means if something or someone grows on us, we start to like them more.

Example: Scientists and doctors alike have jumped on the bandwagon.

Hence, the correct option is (C).

Ques (1-19):Direction: In the following question, out of the given alternatives, choose the one which can be substituted for the given sentence.

Q.1 "Being afraid of water or being near water"
[SSC Sub Inspector (CPO), 2018], [SSC Sub Inspector (CPO), 2017]

A. Xenophobia **B.** Autophobia
C. Monophobia **D.** Aquaphobia

Q.2 "Difficult or impossible to reach or to get"
[SSC Sub Inspector (CPO), 2018], [SSC Sub Inspector (CPO), 2017]

A. Illegible **B.** Inevitable
C. Inaudible **D.** Inaccessible

Q.3 The scientific study of the mind
[SSC Sub Inspector (CPO), 2018], [SSC Sub Inspector (CPO), 2017]

A. Philology **B.** Psychology
C. Sociology **D.** Anthropology

Q.4 A place where ships load and unload goods
[SSC Sub Inspector (CPO), 2018], [SSC Sub Inspector (CPO), 2017]

A. Port **B.** Terminal **C.** Coach **D.** Hangar

Q.5 One who studies human antiquities
[SSC Sub Inspector (CPO), 2018], [SSC Sub Inspector (CPO), 2017]

A. Apologist **B.** Anthropologist
C. Archaeologist **D.** Entomologist

Q.6 Something that is real or actual, rather than imaginary.
A. Vague **B.** Elusive
C. Tangible **D.** Imperceptible

Q.7 A contest between two people to settle a point of honour
A. Dual **B.** Duel **C.** Duo **D.** Duet

Q.8 A speech made to oneself
A. Soliloquy **B.** Solitary
C. Eloquent **D.** Dialogue

Q.9 An area of grassland where animals graze
[SSC MTS, 2019]

A. Forest **B.** Park **C.** Meadow **D.** Garden

Q.10 A solution or remedy for all difficulties or diseases
A. Riddle **B.** Panacea
C. Ailment **D.** Dilemma

Q.11 Showing great knowledge that is based on careful study
A. Amateurish **B.** Inexperienced
C. Erudite **D.** Untrained

Q.12 Without risk of punishment
[Territorial Army Officer, 2019]

A. Impudent **B.** Impunity
C. Inexorable **D.** Imperturbable

Q.13 A song embodying religious and sacred emotions
A. Ballad **B.** Lyrics **C.** Ode **D.** Hymn

Q.14 Extreme old age when a man behaves like a child
A. Imbecility **B.** Senility
C. Dotage **D.** Superannuation

Q.15 The practice or art of choosing, cooking, and eating good food
A. Idolatry **B.** Horticulture
C. Hydrophobia **D.** Gastronomy

Q.16 A person or thing living or existing at the same time as another
A. Cynic **B.** Predator
C. Fanatic **D.** Contemporary

Q.17 Impossible to satisfy
A. Vulnerable **B.** Potable
C. Insatiable **D.** Opaque

Q.18 A child born after the death of its father
A. Posthumous **B.** Theist
C. Notorious **D.** Pedestrian

Q.19 A person hurt or killed in an accident
A. Casualty **B.** Martyr **C.** Patient **D.** Injured

Ques (20-30):

Direction: In the following question, out of the given alternatives, choose the one which can be substituted for the given sentence.

Q.20 A large bundle bound for storage or transportation
A. Bevy **B.** Bouquet **C.** Bale **D.** Brood

Q.21 A fault that may be forgiven
A. Veteran **B.** Versatile **C.** Venial **D.** Virgin

Q.22 Something causing shock or dismay
A. Mischievous **B.** Remarkable
C. Frivolous **D.** Appalling

Q.23 A song sung at a burial
A. Hymn **B.** Dirge **C.** Ballad **D.** Sonnet

Q.24 Something happening by chance in a happy and beneficial way
A. Serendipity **B.** Serenity
C. Misadventure **D.** Serendipity

Q.25 A long or roundabout route that is taken to avoid something
A. Excursion **B.** Rambling
C. Divergence **D.** Detour

Q.26 One skilled in telling stories

A. Ventral **B.** Fanatic

C. Raconteur **D.** Tyro

Q.27 Fear of Fire

A. Arsonphobia **B.** Astraphobia

C. Astrophobia **D.** Arrhenphobia

Q.28 Critical judge of any art and craft

A. Comrade **B.** Curator

C. Connoisseur **D.** Crusader

Q.29 Open refusal to obey orders

A. Obedience **B.** Adherence

C. Defiance **D.** Compliance

Q.30 Incapable of making mistakes

A. Negligible **B.** Infallible

C. Inevitable **D.** Ineligible

// Smart Answer Sheet //

Correct Indicates percentage of students who answered questions correctly.

Skipped Indicates percentage of students who skipped questions.

Q.	Ans.	Correct	Skipped
1	D	67.03 %	32.32 %
2	D	49.08 %	32.66 %
3	B	51.56 %	44.25 %
4	A	50.62 %	30.78 %
5	C	59.49 %	34.02 %
6	C	48.3 %	34.86 %
7	B	69.43 %	30.33 %
8	A	52.38 %	36.48 %
9	C	45.05 %	52.49 %
10	B	67.38 %	32.14 %
11	C	62.66 %	37.27 %
12	B	60.3 %	30.1 %
13	D	65.01 %	32.4 %
14	B	56.09 %	40.5 %
15	D	46.37 %	36.32 %
16	D	43.95 %	39.39 %
17	C	45.65 %	39.71 %
18	A	48.52 %	32.53 %
19	A	45.66 %	48.65 %
20	C	54.87 %	32.5 %
21	C	46.17 %	44.12 %
22	D	60.84 %	38.68 %
23	B	51.64 %	37.39 %
24	A	58.02 %	35.11 %
25	D	43.53 %	32.33 %
26	C	41.41 %	49.75 %
27	A	52.92 %	38.18 %
28	C	54.47 %	30.89 %
29	C	52.28 %	45.46 %
30	B	49.7 %	45.11 %

Performance Analysis	
Avg. Score (%)	46.67%
Toppers Score (%)	60.0%
Your Score	

//Hints and Solutions//

1. The word 'Aquaphobia' means 'an abnormal fear of water.'

Example: She has aquaphobia so she didn't go near the swimming pool.

The root word 'phobia' means 'an irrational fear of something that's unlikely to cause harm' and the root word 'aqua' means 'water'.

Hence, the correct option is (D).

2. The word 'inaccessible' means 'very difficult or impossible to travel to or reach or obtain'.

Examples:

1. This is one of the most **inaccessible** places in the world.
2. Some of the houses on the hillside are **inaccessible** to cars.

Hence, the correct option is (D).

3. The word 'Psychology' means 'the scientific study of the human mind and its functions, especially those affecting behavior in a given context.'

Eg. She had an undergraduate degree in **psychology**.

Hence, the correct option is (B).

4. The word 'Port' means 'an area of water and the land and buildings surrounding it, where ships can take on and off goods and passengers.'

Eg. We had a good view of all the ships coming into/leaving **port**.

Hence, the correct option is (A).

5. The word 'Archaeologist' means 'someone who studies the buildings, graves, tools and other objects of people who lived in the past.'

Example: The site of the temple was discovered by a group of archaeologists.

Hence, the correct option is (C).

6. Tangible means something that is real or actual, rather than imaginary.

- Vague means which is not clear.
- Elusive means difficult to describe.
- Imperceptible means difficult to perceive by mind or senses.

Hence, the correct option is (C).

7. Duel: combat between two persons specifically.

- Dual: consisting of two parts, elements, or aspects.
- Duo: a pair of people or things, especially in music or entertainment
- Duet: a performance by two singers, instrumentalists, or dancers.

Hence, the correct option is (B).

8. Soliloquy: an act of speaking one's thoughts aloud when by oneself or regardless of any hearers, especially by a character in a play.

- Solitary: done or existing alone.
- Eloquent: fluent or persuasive in speaking or writing.
- Dialogue: a conversation between two or more people as a feature of a book, play, or film.

Hence, the correct option is (A).

9. Meadow: an area of land with grass and other wild plants in it and is a natural grassland, used for grazing animals.

- Forest: a large area of land covered with trees and plants, usually larger than wood, or the trees and plants themselves.
- Park: a large area of land with grass and trees which is maintained for the pleasure of the public.
- Garden: a piece of land, usually in a yard next to a house, where you grow flowers and vegetables

Hence, the correct option is (C).

10. A solution or remedy for all difficulties or diseases is called a panacea.

Example: Technology is not a panacea for all our problems.

Hence, the correct option is (B).

11. Erudite means having or showing great knowledge or learning.

- Amateurish means done in an unskilful or inept way.
- Inexperienced means having little knowledge or experience of a particular thing.
- Untrained means not made adept or expert by instruction or experience.

Hence, the correct option is (C).

12. Impunity means exemption or freedom from punishment, harm, or loss.

- Impudent means marked by contemptuous or cocky boldness or disregard of others.
- Inexorable means not to be persuaded, moved or stopped.
- Imperturbable means marked by extreme calm, impassivity, and steadiness.

Hence, the correct option is (B).

13. Hymn is a religious song of praise typically a Christian song.

- Ballad is a poem or song narrating a popular story in short stanzas.
- Lyrics is a lyric poem or verse.
- Ode is a lyric poem typically in the form of an address.

Hence, the correct option is (D).

14. Senility means showing poor mental ability because of old age, especially being unable to think clearly and make decisions.

Therefore, by the definition, we can infer that senility is the correct one-word substitute.

Hence, the correct option is (B).

15. Gastronomy is the practice or art of choosing, cooking, and eating good food.

- Idolatry is extreme admiration and love for something or someone.
- Horticulture is the practice of garden cultivation and management.
- Hydrophobia is an extreme fear of water especially because of a symptom of rabies.

Hence, the correct option is (D).

16. A person or thing living or existing at the same time as another is known as contemporary.

- A cynic is a person who questions whether something will happen or whether it is worthwhile.
- A predator is a person who ruthlessly exploits others.
- A fanatic is a person filled with excessive and single-minded zeal.

Hence, the correct option is (D).

17. The word 'insatiable' refers to (an appetite or desire) impossible to satisfy.

- Vulnerable means exposed to the possibility of being attacked or harmed.
- Potable means safe to drink or drinkable.
- Opaque means not able to be seen through or not transparent.

Hence, the correct option is (C).

18. The word 'posthumous' refers to (of a child) born after the death of its father.

- Theist is a person who believes in the existence of a god or gods.
- Notorious means famous or well known, typically for some bad quality or deed.
- A Pedestrian is a person walking rather than traveling in a vehicle.

Hence, the correct option is (A).

19. Casualty means a person killed or injured in a war or accident.

- Martyr is a person who is killed because of their religious or other beliefs.
- Patient is a person receiving or registered to receive medical treatment.
- Injured means harmed, damaged, or impaired.

Hence, the correct option is (A).

20. Bale: a large quantity of something pressed tightly together and tied up

Example: When the storm arose on the river, they had to bale out to reach the shore safely.

- Bevy: a large group of people or things of a particular kind
- Bouquet: a bunch of flowers that are arranged in an attractive way
- Brood: to worry, or to think a lot about something that makes you worried or sad

Hence, the correct option is (C).

21. Venial means a fault that may be forgiven.

- Veteran means one, who has a long experience in any occupation.
- Versatile means interested in and clever at many different things.
- Virgin means a woman who has no sexual experience.

Hence, the correct option is (C).

22. Appalling means something causing shock or dismay.

For example: She suffered appalling injuries in the accident.

- Mischievous means causing or showing a fondness for causing trouble in a playful way.
- Remarkable means worthy of attention; striking.
- Frivolous means not having any serious purpose or value.

Hence, the correct option is (D).

23. Dirge: Refers to a song that is sung, lamenting for the dead, especially at their funeral.

- Hymn: Refers to a religious song sung in the praise of God.
- Ballad: Refers to a short story that is narrated using short stanzas.
- Sonnet: Refers to a single stanza poem

Hence, the correct option is (B).

24. Serendipity means the occurrence and development of events by chance in a happy or beneficial way.

For eg; It was a fortunate incident of serendipity.

Hence, the correct option is (A).

25. Detour means a long or roundabout route that is taken to avoid something or to visit somewhere along the way. For example: 'When we travel further along the road to Foca, and take a detour into the Treskavica mountains, it is easier to see what she means. '

Hence, the correct option is (D).

26. Raconteur means a person who tells anecdotes in a skillful and amusing way. In other words, a person who can make a story about his day absolutely hilarious is an example of a raconteur. A storyteller, especially a person noted for telling stories with skill and wit.

Hence, the correct option is (C).

27. Arsonphobia is the fear of fire. People who have this fear would avoid things such as bar-b-ques, campfires, fire pits, lighters, matches, etc. Arsonphobia refers to the irrational fear of fire. Fire is a symbol of destruction and people suffers from this phobia feels the same in the literal meaning.

Hence, the correct option is (A).

28. Connoisseur means a person who has a great deal of knowledge about the fine arts, cuisines, or an expert judge in matters of taste.

For example: He was a man of wide knowledge, a connoisseur in art and music.

Hence, the correct option is (C).

29. Defiance: open resistance; bold disobedience.

- Obedience: compliance with an order, request, or law or submission to another's authority.
- Adherence: attachment or commitment to a person, cause, or belief.
- Compliance: the action or fact of complying with a wish or command.

Hence, the correct option is (C).

30. Infallible never wrong, failing, or making a mistake

Example: Even the experts are not infallible.

- Negligible too slight or small in amount to be of importance
- Inevitable certain to happen and unable to be avoided or prevented
- Ineligible not allowed to do or have something, according to particular rules

Hence, the correct option is (B).

Ques (1-4):Direction: The question below consists of a set of labelled sentences. Out of the four options given, select the most logical order of the sentences to form a coherent paragraph.

Q.1 P - A Non-performing asset (NPA) is defined as a credit facility in respect of which the interest and/or installment of Bond finance principal has remained 'past due' for a specified period of time.

Q - Once the borrower has failed to make interest or principal payments for 90 days the loan is considered to be a non-performing asset.

R - 'Non Performing Assets' have been in the news recently.

S - It must be noted, Non-performing assets are problematic for financial institutions since they depend on interest payments for income.

A. RSPQ **B.** RPQS **C.** RQSP **D.** RPSQ

Q.2 P - More and more people are becoming conscious about their health.

Q - These advertisements highlight the nutritional value and health benefits of the products.

R - This is why a lot of food processing companies are coming out with health-specific products.

S - Further, to promote such products, specific advertisements are being made.

A. PQRS **B.** PRSQ **C.** PSRQ **D.** PRQS

Q.3 P - It further escalates exponentially with the burning of firecrackers on major festivals at this time.

Q - The problem of smog in Delhi just as winter sets in has become alarming in the last few years.

R - Heeding to such requests, the Supreme Court has decided to fix a time period beyond which burning of firecrackers will not be allowed.

S - Environmental organizations have requested for a partial ban on burning of firecrackers.

A. QRPS **B.** QPSR **C.** PRSQ **D.** PRQS

Q.4 P - On Tuesday, the Early Warning System (EWS) picked up the disturbance in the sea.

Q - On Wednesday, the Meteorological Department issued a public warning and alerted the media.

R - However, the cyclone did not reach the landmass, so no destruction was observed.

S - This disturbance hinted at the possibility of a low-pressure wind system which could turn into a cyclone.

A. PSQR **B.** PRSQ **C.** PQSR **D.** PSRQ

Ques (5-8):Direction: In the following question, sentences of a paragraph have been jumbled and labeled as A, B, C and D. You are required to rearrange the jumbled sentences of the paragraph and mark your response accordingly by selecting the correct option.

Q.5 A. Before the 12th century, It is to be identified as Carnatic classical music.

B. And has been evolving since the 12th century.

C. It is a tradition that originated in Vedic ritual chants.

D. Shastriya Sangeet is the classical music of North India.

A. DCBA **B.** DCAB **C.** ABCD **D.** ABDC

Q.6 A. "It is mine. I saw it first," claimed one cat.

B. Suddenly they spotted a loaf of bread lying beneath a tree.

C. Once upon a time, two cats were passing through a street.

D. Both pounced upon it and caught the loaf at the same time.

A. ADBC **B.** BADC **C.** DBCA **D.** CBDA

Q.7 A. It is one of the most popular pastimes.

B. Finding fault with others is the most common human folly.

C. But while railing at others, we hardly realize that we have the same faults in ourselves.

D. We like to sit in idle groups and rail about the shortcomings of others.

A. DBCA **B.** CBDA **C.** BADC **D.** ADBC

Q.8 A. She understood my signs, and I could make her do as I wished.

B. My constant companion was Martha, our cook's daughter.

C. We even helped in feeding the hens which crowded around the kitchen steps.

D. This pleased me greatly and we spent a lot of time together.

A. BADC **B.** CBDA **C.** DCAB **D.** ADCB

Ques (9-13):Directions: Given below are four sentences in jumbled order. Pick the option that gives their correct order.

Q.9 A. But it does not appear to have any effect on the children.

B. School teachers try to do their best from the early years by ordering, "Silence!" every few seconds in the class.

C. They look sweet and elegant but the moment they open their mouths, they let out a shattering volume of sound.

D. Someone noted recently that present-day babies are peculiarly loud-throated.

A. DCBA **B.** ACBD **C.** CABD **D.** BACD

Q.10 A. Soon after they left school, they decided that a small town was no place to make a fortune.

B. On reaching Paris, they agreed to separate because they wished to be independent of each other.

C. So, they ran away from home and managed to reach France on a cargo ship.

D. My father was a year older than his brother Oscar.

A. ACBD **B.** BDCA **C.** DBAC **D.** DACB

Q.11 A. Mahatma Gandhi got a doctor to volunteer his services for six months.

B. Health conditions in Champaran were miserable.

C. The doctor gave quinine to malaria patients and the ointment with castor oil to those with skin eruptions.

D. Only three medicines were available- castor oil, quinine and sulphur ointment.

A. BADC **B.** BCDA **C.** ACBD **D.** CDAB

Q.12 A. Dr. Prince became aware of a small figure standing in the aisle beside his seat.

B. "Won't your mother be wondering where you are?" he asked her.

C. He brought his eyes into focus and saw that it was a girl of seven or eight.

D. She was staring at him steadily with large blue eyes.

A. ACDB **B.** BDAC **C.** CDBA **D.** ABCD

Q.13 A. She could not accompany her daughter due to visa restrictions.

B. That trip to Florida with her father Yuri launched her on the path to success.

C. Maria had not yet celebrated her tenth birthday when she was packed off in a train to the United States.

D. But it also required a heart-wrenching two-year separation from her mother Yelena.

A. CADB **B.** BCAD **C.** CBDA **D.** ABCD

Ques (14-16):Direction: In the following question, sentences of a paragraph have been jumbled and labeled as A, B, C and D. You are required to rearrange the jumbled sentences of the paragraph and mark your response accordingly by selecting the correct option.

Q.14 A: For them it is the emotions.

B: For them happiness is not at all proportional to their income but their attitude towards life.

C: Which decide whether the person is happy or unhappy.

D: There are large number of people whose basic physical needs are easily satisfied.

A. DCBA **B.** ABCD **C.** DACB **D.** ACBD

Q.15 A: After inspection the two would stand up.

B: Once a week Pratham led Heera, the elephant, down to river.

C: The elephant lay down on Pratham's side, then he looked at his feet and examined his whole body for sores.

D: The elephant knew it was time to return. So, both the elephant and trainer would return home.

A. BCAD **B.** ADCB **C.** DCBA **D.** ACDB

Q.16 A: We feel deeply hurt when a friend says sharply, "I can't talk to you right now".

B: A friend's rudeness is much more damaging than a stranger's as it hurts us instead of making angry.

C: Or when a friend shows up late for a meeting with no valid reason, we get a little sad.

D: In these situations, we feel that we are being taken for granted.

A. CBDA **B.** BACD **C.** ADCB **D.** DBCA

Q.17 Direction: Examine the four jumbled sentences. Out of the given options, pick the one that gives their correct order.

A. Next, keep tapping the pot on all sides and at the bottom until the plant loosens.

B. Finally, slide the plant gently and remove the old potting mix on a newspaper.

C. The first thing to do when repotting is to remove the plant from the current pot.

D. Begin by holding the plant gently, and turning the pot sideways.

A. BDAC **B.** CDAB **C.** DBCA **D.** ACDB

Q.18 Direction: Arrange the jumbled sentences to make a meaningful paragraph.

A. Half the world's population is now under lockdown orders.

B. As more information about the virus has become available, public advisories have also shapeshifted accordingly.

C. It is to help fight the Covid-19 contagion that has picked up fearful pace through the month of March.

D. One such evolution has taken place on the question of masks.

A. ADBC **B.** ACBD **C.** ABCD **D.** ACDB

Q.19 Direction: In the following question, sentences of a paragraph have been jumbled and labeled as A, B, C and D. You are required to rearrange the jumbled sentences of the paragraph and mark your response accordingly by selecting the correct option.

A: The opposite of demonetization is remonetization, in which a form of payment is restored as legal tender.

B: Sometimes, a country completely replaces the old currency with a new currency.

C: The current form or forms of money is pulled from circulation and retired, often to be replaced with new notes or coins.

D: Demonetization is the act of stripping a currency unit of its status as legal tender.

A. DCBA **B.** DCAB **C.** DBCA **D.** ADCB

Q.20 Direction: In the following question, sentences of a paragraph have been jumbled and labeled as A, B, C and D. You are required to rearrange the jumbled sentences of the paragraph and mark your response accordingly by selecting the correct option.

A. Transporting substances to and from our cells is a major function of blood.

B. Providing immunity and protection against bacteria and viruses is also another function of blood.

C. Blood is a component of the cardiovascular system.

D. It is composed of blood cells and an aqueous fluid known as plasma.

A. ADCB **B.** DCAB **C.** CDAB **D.** BCAD

Q.21 Direction: Arrange these parts so as to form a complete meaningful sentence/paragraph and then choose the correct combination.

A : disintegrates some part of the old truths, and

B : there by upsets the way of men's thinking and the ways of their lives

C : science does not merely add new truths to the old ones, but

D : sometimes the new truth it discovers

Which of the sequences present the most logical sentence?

A. ACBD **B.** CDAB **C.** ABCD **D.** CBAD

Q.22 Direction: In the following question, sentences of a paragraph have been jumbled and labeled as A, B, C and D. You are required to rearrange the jumbled sentences of the paragraph and mark your response accordingly by selecting the correct option.

A. The element symbol for Plutonium is Pu, rather than Pl.

B. They later withdrew it as they realized it could also be used for an atomic bomb.

C. The researchers submitted the proposed name and symbol to the journal Physical Review.

D. This is because Pu was a more amusing symbol of the two.

A. DCAB **B.** ADCB **C.** CDAB **D.** BCAD

Q.23 Directions: Given below are four sentences in jumbled order. Select the option that gives their correct order.

A. This flight takes place on a hot summer day.

B. It has a pair of wings but bites them off after its 'wedding' flight.

C. In the heat, the queen leaves the nest and goes out to meet a drone, high up in the air.

D. The queen is the mother of the entire population of a colony of ants.

A. DBAC **B.** BACD **C.** CABD **D.** ACBD

Q.24 Directions: Given below are four sentences in jumbled order. Pick the option that gives their correct order.

A. Someone had been smart enough to remove it before I went on the rampage.

B. My hands had been itching to tear down that collage from my bedroom wall.

C. But I found the wall bare.

D. So, I entered my room in a hurry.

A. DABC **B.** CBAD **C.** ABCD **D.** BDCA

Q.25 Directions: In the following question, sentences of a paragraph have been jumbled and labelled as A, B, C, and D. You are required to rearrange the jumbled sentences of the paragraph and mark your response accordingly by selecting the correct option.

A: The Bihar Legislative Assembly election will be held to elect members of the Legislative Assembly of the Indian State of Bihar.

B: Finally, he results will be announced on 10 November 2020.

C: The elections will be conducted amid the COVID-19 pandemic with the necessary guidelines issued by the Election Commission of India.

D: The election will be held in three phases for a total of 243 seats.

A. ACDB **B.** CABD **C.** DCAB **D.** ADCB

Q.26 Directions: Sentences of a paragraph are given below in jumbled order. Arrange the sentences in the right order to form a meaningful and coherent paragraph.

A. But the eagle, in wrath, gave the beetle a flap of his wing, and straightaway seized upon the hare and devoured him.

B. The beetle, therefore, interceded with the eagle, begging of him not to kill the poor suppliant, and pleaded with him not to kill so small an animal.

C. When the eagle flew away, the beetle flew after him, to learn where his nest was.

D. A hare, being pursued by an eagle, took himself for refuge to the nest of a beetle, whom he begged to save him.

A. ACDB **B.** DCAB **C.** CBAD **D.** DBAC

Q.27 Directions: In the following question, sentences of a paragraph have been jumbled and labelled as A, B, C and D. You are required to rearrange the jumbled sentences of the paragraph and mark your response accordingly by selecting the correct option.

A: According to BCCI, the 2015 IPL season contributed ₹11.5 billion (US$160 million) to the GDP of the Indian economy.

B: The Indian Premier League (IPL) is a Twenty20 cricket league in India contested by eight teams representing eight different cities or states in India.

C: The IPL has an exclusive window in ICC Future Tours Programme.

D: The league was founded by the Board of Control for Cricket in India (BCCI) in 2008.

A. BACD **B.** ACDB **C.** BDCA **D.** CBDA

Q.28 Directions: In the following question, sentences of a paragraph have been jumbled and labelled as A, B, C and D. You are required to rearrange the jumbled sentences of the paragraph and mark your response accordingly by selecting the correct option.

A: Thirdly, printing helped in the dissemination of knowledge in a permanent form.

B: However, all these are passive media.

C: Speech was the first means of conveying ideas followed by writing as a means for storing information.

D: Computer is the only medium that cannot only store but analyze information to make decisions—therefore it is called the fourth information revolution.

A. ACDB **B.** CABD **C.** BDCA **D.** DACB

Q.29 Directions: The question below comprises four scattered segments of a paragraph. Identify from among the four choices the sequences that correctly assemble the segments and complete the paragraph.

A. Mr D Gautam's personality sets him apart the rest.

B. Nothing is too small for his attention

C. He has a fanatical devotion to detail.

D. This is what makes him a different guy.

[SBI Clerk, 2020]

A. ACBD **B.** ABCD **C.** BDCA **D.** DCBA

Q.30 Directions: Given below are four jumbled sentences. Select the option that gives their correct order.

A. Far below he saw green meadows and in their midst a village.

B. He sat down and rested in the shadow of a rock.

C. Nunez was in a pass between the mountains.

D. He slowly climbed down the precipices and about midday came to the plain, stiff and tired out.

A. ADBC **B.** CADB **C.** CDAB **D.** ABDC

// Smart Answer Sheet //

Correct Indicates percentage of students who answered questions correctly.

Skipped Indicates percentage of students who skipped questions.

Q.	Ans.	Correct	Skipped
1	B	67.59 %	32.18 %
2	B	45.46 %	51.15 %
3	B	44.55 %	50.94 %
4	A	52.16 %	34.77 %
5	A	53.44 %	43.02 %
6	D	64.73 %	30.96 %
7	C	62.7 %	30.09 %
8	A	45.91 %	45.75 %
9	A	52.58 %	32.72 %
10	D	47.53 %	49.88 %
11	A	46.93 %	41.03 %
12	A	67.04 %	30.41 %
13	C	60.4 %	30.09 %
14	C	52.07 %	38.63 %
15	A	65.33 %	30.81 %
16	B	63.14 %	32.49 %
17	B	55.76 %	31.91 %
18	B	60.69 %	37.58 %
19	A	66.08 %	31.47 %
20	C	65.64 %	32.73 %
21	B	49.5 %	48.19 %
22	B	44.84 %	36.31 %
23	A	42.19 %	36.24 %
24	D	56.91 %	35.83 %
25	D	65.63 %	30.37 %
26	D	44.92 %	31.66 %
27	C	51.57 %	44.56 %
28	B	40.1 %	57.76 %
29	A	54.45 %	31.14 %
30	B	53.35 %	34.72 %

Performance Analysis	
Avg. Score (%)	33.33%
Toppers Score (%)	70.0%
Your Score	

//Hints and Solutions//

1. The first sentence should ideally highlight a subject that is being discussed by the sentences that form a passage.

In sentence R, the use of the phrase 'in the news recently' highlight that it should be the opening sentence and at the same time introduces the subject i.e. 'Non-performing assets'.

Further, the subject is detailed by sentence P, therefore it should follow sentence R.

Among Q and S, S uses the concluding phrase 'it must be noted'. Thus, S should be the final sentence and Q should precede it.

Therefore, the correct order should be RPQS.

Hence, the correct option is (B).

2. The first sentence should ideally introduce the topic of discussion/subject.

P - performs this function (highlighting health consciousness to be the topic of discussion) and should, therefore, be the first sentence.

R - through the use of the phrase 'this is why' uses the reason highlighted by P to extend the subject i.e. health-specific products.

Among S and Q, S highlights that specific advertisements are being made and Q then, details the nature of the advertisements.

Thus, Q should follow S.

Therefore, the correct order should be PRSQ.

The ordered paragraph will be:

More and more people are becoming conscious about their health. This is why a lot of food processing companies are coming out with health-specific products. Further, to promote such products, specific advertisements are being made. These advertisements highlight the nutritional value and health benefits of the products.

Hence, the correct option is (B).

3. The first sentence should ideally highlight the topic for discussion/subject.

Q - performs this function i.e. introduces 'smog in Delhi' to be the topic for discussion.

P - is the logical extension of the subject as can be determined through the use of 'further'.

Between S and R, S discusses the 'request by environment organizations' whereas R details the result i.e. 'heeding to such requests...'

Therefore, R should follow S.

Therefore, the correct order after rearrangement will be QPSR.

The ordered paragraph will be:

The problem of smog in Delhi just as winter sets in has become alarming in the last few years. It further escalates exponentially with the burning of firecrackers on major festivals at this time. Environmental organizations have requested for a partial ban on burning of firecrackers. Heeding to such requests, the Supreme Court has decided to fix a time period beyond which burning of firecrackers will not be allowed.

Hence, the correct option is (B).

4. To determine the logical order of this sentence, we must adhere to the chronology of events.

P - Tuesday event, should clearly be first it highlights 'the disturbance' to be the subject.

S - Which details 'this disturbance' is the logical extension of P.

Q - which details the event on Wednesday i.e. public warning should follow S.

And finally, R is the concluding sentence.

Therefore, the correct order after rearrangement is PSQR.

Hence, the correct option is (A).

5. The sentence 'D' is independent of any other sentence as it is giving general information about the noun "Shastriya Sangeet". Therefore, the sentence 'D' is the first part.

The pronoun 'It' mentioned in the sentence 'C' refers back to the noun 'Shastriya Sangeet' mentioned in the sentence 'D'. Therefore, D follows C.

The sentence 'B' haven't any subject, The pronoun 'It' mentioned in the sentence 'C' act as the subject for the sentence 'B'. Therefore, B is the third part.

The sentence 'A' is the concluding sentence. Therefore, it is the last part.

Thus, the correct sequence is: DCBA.

Hence, the correct option is (A).

6. Sentence C introduces us to the subject 'two cats'. It is the introductory sentence and will be put in the first place.

Sentence B tells us about the instance of the cats spotting a loaf of bread. It will be put in second place.

Sentence D tells us the reaction of the cats after seeing the loaf of bread. It will be put in third place.

The last sentence is A as it mentions the conviction of one of the cats that the loaf was hers as she first spotted it.

Thus, the correct sequence is: CBDA.

Hence, the correct option is (D).

7. The sentence 'B' is independent of any other sentences as it is giving general information about "Finding fault with others". Therefore, 'B' is the first part.

The pronoun "It" mentioned in the sentence 'A' refers back to 'finding fault with others' mentioned in the sentence 'B'. Therefore, 'A' follows 'B'.

The phrase "sit in idle groups and rail" mentioned in the sentence 'D' is linked with the "most popular pastimes" mentioned in the sentence 'A'. Therefore, 'D' follows 'A'.

The sentence 'C' is the concluding sentence. Therefore, 'C' is the last sentence.

Thus, the correct sequence is: BADC.

Hence, the correct option is (C).

8. The sentence 'B' is independent of any other sentences as it is giving general information about the noun "Martha". Therefore, 'B' is the first part.

The pronoun "She" mentioned in the sentence 'A' refers back to the noun 'Martha' mentioned in the sentence 'B'. Therefore, 'A' follows 'B'.

The pronoun "we" mentioned in the sentence 'D' refers back to the "author and Martha" mentioned in the sentence 'A'. Therefore, 'D' follows 'A'.

The sentence 'C' is the concluding sentence. Therefore, 'C' is the last sentence.

Thus, the correct sequence is: BADC.

Hence, the correct option is (A).

9. The correct order is "DCBA".

The sentence 'D' is independent of any other sentence as it is giving general information about "present-day babies". So, 'D' is the first part.

The pronoun "they" mentioned in the sentence 'C' refers back to the 'babies' mentioned in the sentence 'D'. So, 'C' follows 'D'.

The word 'Silence!' in the sentence 'B' is linked with the phrase 'shattering volume of sound' mentioned in the sentence 'C'. So, 'B' follows 'C'.

The sentence 'A' is the concluding sentence. So, 'A' is the last sentence.

Hence, the correct option is (A).

10. The correct order is "DACB".

The sentence 'D' is independent of any other sentence as it is giving general information about "My father and his brother". So, 'D' is the first part.

The pronoun "they" mentioned in the sentence 'A' refers back to the 'My father and his brother' mentioned in the sentence 'D'. So, 'A' follows 'D'.

The phrase 'to make a fortune' in the sentence 'A' is linked with the phrase 'they ran away from home' mentioned in the sentence 'C'. So, 'C' follows 'A'.

The sentence 'B' is the concluding sentence. So, 'B' is the last sentence.

Hence, the correct option is (D).

11. The correct order is "BADC".

The sentence 'B' is independent of any other sentences as it is giving general information about "Health conditions in Champaran". So, 'B' is the first part.

The noun "doctor" mentioned in the sentence 'A' is linked with the phrase 'Health conditions' mentioned in the sentence 'B'. So, 'A' follows 'B'.

The noun "quinine" mentioned in the sentence 'C' refers back to the 'quinine' mentioned in the sentence 'D'. So, 'C' follows 'D'.

Hence, the correct option is (A).

12. The correct order is 'ACDB'.

Here, in the given question Only Part A can be the first sentence because it is the start of an incident and 'Dr. Prince is a noun also.

Part C is connected with Part A as Part C describes 'Dr. Prince' saw a girl of seven or eight.

And Part D explains how that girl was staring at him or what she was doing.

Lastly, Part B will be used, because, what 'Dr. Prince' asked that Girl is shown.

Hence, the correct option is (A).

13. The correct order is 'CBDA'.

Part C will be the first sentence. Here, the given question tells 'Maria has not yet celebrated her tenth birthday.' it is the starting of an incident.

Part C tells about 'Maria traveling to the United States'.

And part B further explains her trip. 'She had traveled with her father to Florida'. Therefore, Part C will follow part B.

Part D will be used next because it tells that she had left her mother behind.

Lastly, Part A will be used to explain why her mother could not travel with her.

Hence, the correct option is (C).

14. D is the sentence that establishes the subject matter. Hence, it'll be the first sentence after rearrangement.

A will come after D because it further explains the characteristic of those people.

C is connected to A by 'which'. Which is used to refer to something already mentioned.

B contextually follows C. As it summarizes by stating that happiness is not at all proportional to income.

Thus, the correct arrangement would be: DACB

Hence, the correct option is (C).

15. B is the sentence that introduces the characters 'Pratham' and his elephant 'Heera'. Hence, it will be the first sentence after rearrangement.

C contextually follows B because it states the activities of elephant what it does next.

Third sentence will be A because it mentions what they did after the inspection was over,

D is the concluding sentence of arrangement as here they are returning home after everything is done.

Thus, the correct arrangement would be: BCAD

Hence, the correct option is (A).

16. B is the sentence that establishes the subject matter. Hence, it will be the first sentence after the rearrangement.

A is the logical successor of B as it describes what a friend does that can hurt us.

C connects with A through 'or' and presents another situation where our friends hurt us.

D is the closing sentence because it gives a conclusion- 'we feel taken for granted'.

Thus, the correct arrangement would be: BACD

Hence, the correct option is (B).

17. The correct order is CDAB.

The first thing to do when repotting is to remove the plant from the current pot. Begin by holding the plant gently, and turning the pot sideways. Next, keep tapping the pot on all sides and at the bottom until the plant loosens. Finally, slide the plant gently and remove the old potting mix on a newspaper.

- Option (C) must be the first line as it's already mentioned in the sentence. (The first thing to do)
- Option (D) will be the second, as it's explaining how to start the process. (Begin by holding)
- Option (A) is the third sentence, as it's mentioned what to do next. (Next, keep tapping)
- Option (B) is the last one, as the word 'finally' clearly states the last step. (Finally, slide the plant gently).

Hence, the correct option is (B).

18. The given sentence is an example of a Sentence Jumble.

The first statement of a sentence jumbled question is usually an independent general statement, a noun, a universal fact, the starting of an incident, or it starts with 'most' or 'once'.

Here, Part A will be the first sentence because all the options start with Part A.

Part A tells us that 'Half of the world's population is under lockdown'.

Part C will be the next sentence because Part C tells us how beneficial the lockdown will be and how it will help us to fight the Covid- 19.

Part B will be the next sentence because Part B tells us how 'Public advisories have shaped'.

Lastly, Part D will be used.

Correct Answer: Half the world's population is now under lock down orders. It is to help fight the Covid-19 contagion that has picked up fearful pace through the month of March. As more information about the virus has become available, public advisories have also shape shifted accordingly. One such evolution has taken place on the question of masks.

Hence, the correct option is (B).

19. D is the first sentence because it introduces the subject of demonetization. C further explains how it is carried out. So, C is the continuation of the explanation of the subject introduced in D. C talks of the replacement of the current form of money with new notes using the word 'often'. And B talks of the replacement using the word 'sometimes'. Both the two sentences refer to the replacement of currencies, so, both should be written subsequently, and placing C before B is contextually more meaningful. A is a different point, so, it must come after DCB.

Thus, the correct sequence is: DCBA

Hence, the correct option is (A).

20. When ordering the sentences, it is easier to find the first few and then eliminate the options. The first sentence is always independent and introduces a topic. Here, only sentence C is independent and introduces the topic of 'blood'. So, C must be the first sentence. This order is only given by option (C).

Thus, the correct sequence is: CDAB.

Hence, the correct option is (C).

21. C is the opening part containing the subject because the conjunction at the end of C is but the following sentence must be opposite to D in intent, that is A. But the subject of A is in D so CDAB is the right sequence.

Hence, the correct option is (B).

22. When ordering the sentences, it is easier to find the first few and then eliminate the options. The first sentence is always independent and introduces a topic. Here, only sentence A is independent and introduces the topic of 'Plutonium'. Out of the given options, only option (B) begins with A.

Thus, the correct sequence is: ADCB.

Hence, the correct option is (B).

23. The sentence 'D' is independent of any other sentence as it is giving general information about "the queen of ants". Hence, 'D' is the first part.

Sentence B will come after D because it explains what the queen of ants does with the pair of wings.

Sentence A will come after B because it explains when the wedding flight takes place.

The sentence 'C' is the concluding part because it mentions what the queen of ants does in the heat.

Hence, the correct option is (A).

24. The given sentence is an example of Sentence Jumble.

We know that the first statement of a sentence jumbled question is usually an independent general statement, a noun, a universal fact, starting of an incident, or it starts with 'most' or 'once'.

Part B will be the first sentence because it is the starting of an incident.

Part D will be used next because Part B talks about 'tearing down' of the collage and Part D further tell what the author did to tear down that collage.

Part C will be used next because it further explains what the author found when he entered that room.

Lastly, Part A will be used to give a possible explanation the author thinks of the wall being bare

Hence, the correct option is (D).

25. Sentence 'A' is independent of any other sentences as it is giving general information about the "Bihar Legislative Assembly election". Hence, 'A' is the first sentence.

The 'election' mentioned in the sentence 'D' refers back to the "Bihar election" in the sentence 'A' and is further describing the election. Hence, 'D' follows 'A'.

Sentence 'C' talks about the conduction of the elections according to the guidelines and it follows D.

Sentence 'B' concludes the paragraph by starting with 'finally' and by giving some additional information about the election. It talks about the results. Hence, 'C' makes the last sentence.

Hence, the correct option is (D).

26. The sentence 'D' is independent of any other sentence as it is giving general information about "a hare". Hence, 'D' is the first part.

Sentence B will come after D because it explains how the beetle requested or pleaded with the eagle to not kill the hare.

Sentence A will come after B because it explains whether the eagle killed the hare or not.

The sentence 'C' is the concluding part because it explains what the beetle has done finally when the eagle flew away.

Hence, the correct option is (D).

27. Sentence 'B' is independent of any other sentences as it is giving general information about the "Indian Premier League". Hence, 'B' is the first sentence.

The 'league' mentioned in the sentence 'D' refers back to the "Indian Premier League" in sentence 'B' and is further describing the 'IPL'. Hence, 'D' follows 'B'.

Sentence 'C' is further describing the 'IPL' and is linked with the sentence 'D'. Hence, 'C' follows 'D'.

Sentence 'A' concludes the paragraph by giving some additional information about the revenue generated from the IPL. Hence, 'A' makes the last sentence.

Hence, the correct option is (C).

28. Sentence C establishes the subject matter i.e. the various ways through which information can and has been stored. Hence, it will be the first sentence after rearrangement.

A follows C because in C, we talk about the two modes 'speech' and 'writing'. The third mode is introduced in sentence 'A'.

B connects with A through 'however' which is used to introduce something that contrasts with what is previously said.

D is the concluding sentence of the paragraph as it talks about the 'fourth information revolution'.

Hence, the correct option is (B).

29. The introduction is obviously the first sentence, and then the detail has been talked about making sentence C the second one followed by the sentence continuing the usage of the attention and the detail. And finally, what makes him different from the rest. So, the correct sequence is ACBD.

Hence, the correct option is (A).

30. The sentence 'C' is independent of any other sentences as it is giving general information about "Nunez". Hence, 'C' is the first part.

The pronoun "he" mentioned in the sentence 'A' refers back to the noun "Nunez" mentioned in the sentence 'C'. Hence, 'A' follows 'C'.

The phrase 'came to the plain' mentioned in the sentence 'D' is linked with the phrase 'he saw green meadows' mentioned in the sentence 'A'. Hence, 'D' follows 'A'.

The sentence 'B' is the concluding sentence. Hence, 'B' is the last sentence.

Hence, the correct option is (B).

Ques (1-10):Direction: Read the given passage and answer the questions that follow.

Her name was Sulekha, but since her childhood, everyone had been calling her Bholi, the simpleton. She was the fourth daughter of Ramlal. When she was ten months old, she had fallen off the cot on her head and perhaps it had damaged some part of her brain. That was why she remained a backward child and came to be known as Bholi, the simpleton. At birth, the child was very fair and pretty. But when she was two years old, she had an attack of smallpox. Only the eyes were saved, but the entire body was permanently disfigured by deep black pockmarks. Little Sulekha could not speak till she was five as she was a slow learner, and when at last she learnt to speak, she stammered. The other children often made fun of her and mimicked her. As a result, she talked very little. Ramlal had seven children — three sons and four daughters, and the youngest of them was Bholi. It was a prosperous farmer's household and there was plenty to eat and drink. All the children except Bholi were healthy and strong. The sons had been sent to the city to study in schools and later in colleges. Of the daughters, Radha, the eldest, had already been married. The second daughter Mangla's marriage had also been settled, and when that was done, Ramlal would think of the third, Champa. They were good-looking, healthy girls, and it was not difficult to find bridegrooms for them. But Ramlal was worried about Bholi. She had neither good looks nor intelligence. From her very childhood, Bholi was neglected at home. She was seven years old when Mangla was married. The same year a primary school for girls was opened in their village. The Tehsildar Sahib came to perform its opening ceremony. He said to Ramlal, "As a revenue official you are the representative of the government in the village and so you must set an example to the villagers. You must send your daughters to school." That night when Ramlal consulted his wife, she cried, "Are you crazy? If girls go to school, who will marry them?" But Ramlal had not the courage to disobey the Tehsildar. At last, his wife said, "I will tell you what to do. Send Bholi to school. As it is, there is little chance of her getting married, with her ugly face and lack of sense. Let the teachers at school worry about her."

Q.1 Sulekha came to be called Bholi because she was:

[SSC CGL, 2020]

A. Not very intelligent
B. Fair and pretty
C. Healthy and strong
D. The youngest daughter

Q.2 What did the smallpox attack do to Sulekha?

[SSC CGL, 2020]

A. It made her look ugly.
B. It made her dull.
C. It damaged her speech.
D. It damaged her eyes.

Q.3 At what age did Sulekha damage her brain?

[SSC CGL, 2020]

A. Ten months
B. Five years
C. Seven years
D. Two years

Q.4 Bholi's mother agreed to send her to school because:

[SSC CGL, 2020]

A. She wanted to wash her hands off Bholi
B. She cared for Bholi's well-being
C. Bholi was neglected at home
D. She wanted to educate Bholi

Q.5 Which of these statements is NOT true about Bholi?

[SSC CGL, 2020]

A. She was seven when her eldest sister got married.
B. She was neglected by her family.
C. She was a simpleton.
D. She was healthy and strong.

Q.6 The word 'disfigured' suggests that Bholi's looks were:

[SSC CGL, 2020]

A. Enhanced
B. Impaired
C. Improved
D. Preserved

Q.7 How was Ramlal expected to set an example for the villagers?

[SSC CGL, 2020]

A. By treating Bholi as an equal
B. By marrying off his daughters at an early age
C. By sending his daughters to school
D. By sending his sons to school

Q.8 Who was invited to inaugurate the girls' school?

[SSC CGL, 2020]

A. School Headmaster
B. Revenue official
C. Tehsildar
D. Village head

Q.9 'Backward child' in the passage means:

[SSC CGL, 2020]

A. Belonging to an underprivileged community
B. Mentally challenged
C. Physically challenged
D. Belonging to a poor family

Q.10 Why was Ramlal worried about Bholi?

[SSC CGL, 2020]

A. She was too old to get married.
B. It would be difficult to arrange her marriage.
C. It was difficult to comprehend her speech.
D. She was not willing to get educated.

Ques (11-20):Direction: Read the given passage and answer the questions that follow.

Santiniketan embodies Rabindranath Tagore's vision of a place of learning that is unfettered by religious and regional barriers. Established in 1863 with the aim of helping education go beyond the confines of the classroom, Santiniketan grew into the Visva Bharati University in 1921, attracting some of the most creative minds in the country.

He developed a curriculum that was a unique blend of art, human values and cultural interchange. Even today, in every step, in every brick and in every tree at Santiniketan, one can still feel his presence, his passion, his dedication and his pride in the institution. In 1862, Maharishi Debendranath Tagore, father of Rabindranath, was taking a boat ride through Birbhum, the westernmost corner of Bengal, when he came across a landscape that struck him as the perfect place for meditation. He bought the large tract of land and built a small house and planted some saplings around it. Debendranath Tagore decided to call the place Santiniketan, or the 'abode of peace', because of the serenity it brought to his soul. In 1863, he turned it into a spiritual centre where people from all religions, castes and creeds came and participated in meditation.

In the years that followed, Debendranath's son Rabindranath went on to become one of the most formidable literary forces India has ever produced. He wrote in all literary genres but he was first and foremost a poet. As one of the earliest educators to think in terms of the global village, he envisioned an education that was deeply rooted in one's immediate surroundings but connected to the cultures of the wider world.

Located in the heart of nature, the school aimed to combine education with a sense of obligation towards the larger civic community. Blending the best of western and traditional eastern systems of education, the curriculum revolved organically around nature with classes being held in the open air. Tagore wanted his students to feel free despite being in the formal learning environment of a school because he himself had dropped out of school when he found himself unable to think and felt claustrophobic within the four walls of a classroom. Nature walks and excursions were a part of the curriculum, special attention was paid to natural phenomena and students were encouraged to follow the life cycles of insects, birds and plants.

The rural paradise of Santiniketan, Tagore's erstwhile home, has become a thriving centre of art, education and internationalism over the years.

Q.11 What did Santiniketan initially serve as?

[SSC CGL, 2020]

A. A classroom **B.** A summer house
C. A spiritual centre **D.** A holiday resort

Q.12 Which of these statements about Santiniketan is not true?

[SSC CGL, 2020]

A. Santiniketan is located in the western most part of Bengal.
B. Santiniketan grew into Visva Bharati university.
C. At Santiniketan, classes were held in the open air.
D. Santiniketan was set up by Rabindranath Tagore.

Q.13 The curriculum designed for Santiniketan was a blend of:

[SSC CGL, 2020]

A. Spiritual and religious exchange
B. Science and religion
C. Human values, art and culture
D. Western education and village practices

Q.14 Tagore's 'erstwhile' home means:

[SSC CGL, 2020]

A. Serene abode **B.** Former home
C. Rural retreat **D.** Magnificent house

Q.15 Why did Rabindranath drop out of school?

[SSC CGL, 2020]

A. He found the curriculum too tough.
B. He wanted a formal learning environment.
C. He felt stifled within the classroom.
D. He was not interested in studies.

Q.16 With what aim was Santiniketan established?

[SSC CGL, 2020]

A. To nurture plants, birds and insects
B. To attract the most creative minds
C. To make it the perfect place for meditation
D. To encourage education outside the classroom

Q.17 The word 'unfettered' in the text suggests:

[SSC CGL, 2020]

A. Bound by religious beliefs
B. Free from barriers
C. Outside the classroom
D. Restricted by regional differences

Q.18 When did Santiniketan grow into a university?

[SSC CGL, 2020]

A. In 1922 **B.** In 1863 **C.** In 1921 **D.** In 1862

Q.19 What does the name Santiniketan mean?

[SSC CGL, 2020]

A. Abode of love **B.** Abode of peace
C. Abode of culture **D.** Abode of learning

Q.20 Rabindranath was a 'formidable' literary force. This implies he was:

[SSC CGL, 2020]

A. An orthodox educationist
B. An avid reader of books
C. A wealthy landowner
D. A powerful writer

Ques (21-25):Direction: Read the following passage carefully and answer the question that follows.

The catastrophic monsoon floods in Kerala and parts of Karnataka have revived the debate on whether political expediency trumped science. Seven years ago, the Western

Ghats Ecology Expert Panel issued recommendations for the preservation of the fragile western peninsular region. Madhav Gadgil, who chaired the Union Environment Ministry's WGEEP, has said the recent havoc in Kerala is a consequence of short-sighted policymaking, and warned that Goa may also be in the line of nature's fury. The State governments that are mainly responsible for the Western Ghats — Kerala, Karnataka, Tamil Nadu, Goa and Maharashtra — must go back to the drawing table with the reports of both the Gadgil Committee and the Kasturirangan Committee, which was set up to examine the WGEEP report. The task before them is to initiate correctives to environmental policy decisions. This is not going to be easy, given the need to balance human development pressures with stronger protection of the Western Ghats ecology. The issue of allowing extractive industries such as quarrying and mining to operate is arguably the most contentious. A way out could be to create the regulatory framework that was proposed by the Gadgil panel, in the form of an apex Western Ghats Ecology Authority and the State-level units, under the Environment (Protection) Act, and to adopt the zoning system that it proposed. This can keep incompatible activities out of the Ecologically Sensitive Zones (ESZs).

At issue in the Western Ghats — spread over 1,29,037 sq km according to the WGEEP estimate and 1,64,280 sq km as per the Kasturirangan panel — is the calculation of what constitutes the sensitive core and what activities can be carried out there. The entire system is globally acknowledged as a biodiversity hotspot. But population estimates for the sensitive zones vary greatly, based on interpretations of the ESZs. In Kerala, for instance, one expert assessment says 39 lakh households are in the ESZs outlined by the WGEEP, but the figure drops sharply to four lakh households for a smaller area of zones identified by the Kasturirangan panel. The goal has to be sustainable development for the Ghats as a whole. The role of big hydroelectric dams, built during an era of rising power demand and deficits, must now be considered afresh and proposals for new ones dropped. Other low-impact forms of green energy led by solar power are available. A moratorium on quarrying and mining in the identified sensitive zones, in Kerala and also other States, is necessary to assess their environmental impact. Kerala's Finance Minister, Thomas Isaac, has acknowledged the need to review decisions affecting the environment, in the wake of the floods. Public consultation on the expert reports that includes people's representatives will find greater resonance now, and help chart a sustainable path ahead.

Q.21 Which among the following has been attributed by the experts as a reason of the recent floods in Kerala and Karnataka?

A. The states do not have proper system in place of drainage and that is why the rain water always overflows in these two states.

B. The states have no idea how to manage any kind of natural calamity and that is why they cannot tackle any situation however small it may be.

C. The states should be entrusted with the responsibility of protection of environment in the areas within their jurisdiction.

D. The political decision making strategy has always taken the upper hand as compared to the real interests of the environment.

Q.22 According to the passage, the states affected by the floods should do which among the following to prevent such incidents in the future?

A. The states should devote more funds towards the reduction of natural calamities in the states.

B. The states should put in place proper warning mechanism so that the government can get to know the possibility of any natural calamity beforehand.

C. The states should plan properly so that they can implement the recommendations of the expert panels regarding the preservation of the Western Ghats Area.

D. The states should not do anything at present and should only focus on the idea of going all out in disaster management operations.

Q.23 Which among the following is the main issue pointed out in the passage in the implementation of the expert panel reports in various states?

A. There is no proper framework depicted in the expert panel reports to regulate the Ecologically Sensitive Zone in the Western Ghat Area.

B. There is no issue pertaining to the Western Ghat area but the main problem is that the governments do not have enough funds.

C. The reservoirs in the vicinity of the area will spell the doom for the area since they will exhaust the groundwater available in the area.

D. The balance between development and preservation should be there in order to develop the area properly.

Q.24 Which among the following should be the objective of all concerned regarding the development of the Western Ghats Area?

A. The development plan should be well supported by money and also manpower by all the states.

B. The development plan must be drawn up correctly at the first place since it will help gain an upper hand in the whole process.

C. The states should take the development of the Western Ghats region seriously so that the area is actually preserved.

D. The Western Ghats Area should be preserved properly so that there is sustainable development of the area.

Q.25 Which among the following should be the course of action of the government in order to ensure that the Western Ghats Area is preserved properly?

I. There should be utilization of various clean sources of energy such as the solar power in the area

II. There should not be any restriction in mining activities as well as quarrying activities in the area

III. There should not be new construction of hydroelectric dams in the area from now onwards

A. Both I and II **B.** Only II

C. Both I and III **D.** Only I

Ques (26-30):Direction: Read the following passage carefully and answer the question given below it.

I have three visions for India. In 3000 years of our history people from all over the world have come and invaded us, captured our lands, conquered our minds. From Alexander onwards the Greeks, the Turks, the Moguls, the Portuguese, the British, the French, the Dutch, all of them came and looted us, took over what was ours. Yet we have not done this to any other nation. We have not conquered anyone. We have not grabbed their land, their culture, and their history and tried to enforce our way of life on them. Why? Because we respect the freedom of others.

That is why my first vision is that of FREEDOM. I believe that India got its first vision of this in 1857 when we started the war of Independence. It is this freedom that we must protect and nurture and build on. If we are not free, no one will respect us. We have a 10 percent growth rate in most areas. Our poverty levels are falling. Our achievements are being globally recognized today. Yet we lack the self-confidence to see ourselves as a developed nation, self-reliant and self-assured. Isn't this incorrect? My second vision for India is DEVELOPMENT. For fifty years we have been a developing nation. It is time we see ourselves as a developed nation. We are among the top five nations in the world in terms of GDP.

I have a THIRD VISION. India must stand up to the world. Because I believe that unless India stands up to the world, no one will respect us. Only strength respects strength. We must be strong not only as a military power but also as an economic power. Both must go hand-in-hand. My good fortune was to have worked with three great minds. Dr. Vikram Sarabhai, of the Dept. of Space, Professor Satish Dhawan, who succeeded him, and Dr. Brahm Prakash, father of nuclear material. I was lucky to have worked with all three of them closely and consider this the great opportunity of my life.

I was in Hyderabad giving this lecture when a 14-year-old girl asked me for my autograph. I asked her what her goal in life is. She replied: I want to live in a developed India. For her, you and I will have to build this developed India. You must proclaim India is not an underdeveloped nation; it is a highly developed nation. You say that our government is inefficient. You say that our laws are too old. You say that the municipality does not pick up the garbage. You say that the phones don't work, the railways are a joke, the airline is the worst in the world, and mails never reach their destination. You say that our country has been fed to the dogs and is the absolute pits.

Q.26 Who has been termed as the father of nuclear material?

A. Dr. Vikram Sarabhai
B. Dr. Brahm Prakash
C. Professor Satish Dhawan
D. Dr. APJ Abdul Kalam

Q.27 What according to Dr. Kalam should an Indian proclaim while talking about India?

A. India is an underdeveloped nation
B. India is a highly developed nation
C. India is economically grown up, and is no longer an underdeveloped nation
D. India is a super power is technology

Q.28 Dr. Kalam feels that India should be strong in ______.

A. communicative skills
B. economically sound policies
C. military power and economic power
D. missile technology

Q.29 Which of the following is the positive quality of Indians?

A. They are self-centered
B. They are progressive
C. They are shy
D. They have belief in freedom for all

Q.30 A country's development depends on ______.

A. the effective governance
B. meticulous planning
C. committed citizens with the sense of rights and duties together
D. physical facilities

// Smart Answer Sheet //

Correct Indicates percentage of students who answered questions correctly.

Skipped Indicates percentage of students who skipped questions.

Q.	Ans.	Correct	Skipped
1	A	47.28 %	48.06 %
2	A	54.33 %	40.06 %
3	A	64.56 %	31.67 %
4	A	47.94 %	48.2 %
5	D	50.9 %	32.25 %
6	B	43.96 %	44.68 %
7	C	40.48 %	51.44 %
8	C	67.34 %	31.0 %
9	B	55.37 %	35.56 %
10	B	49.32 %	44.94 %
11	C	67.36 %	31.81 %
12	D	62.27 %	34.45 %
13	C	44.72 %	45.17 %
14	B	51.25 %	30.67 %
15	C	50.58 %	33.81 %
16	D	50.92 %	41.96 %
17	B	59.98 %	31.4 %
18	C	68.56 %	30.65 %
19	B	69.0 %	30.91 %
20	D	66.99 %	32.42 %
21	D	43.24 %	52.64 %
22	C	66.04 %	30.56 %
23	D	63.56 %	30.43 %
24	D	60.52 %	37.07 %
25	C	67.88 %	30.8 %
26	B	62.45 %	32.1 %
27	B	45.33 %	51.69 %
28	C	41.99 %	32.93 %
29	D	68.14 %	30.61 %
30	C	59.63 %	36.06 %

Performance Analysis	
Avg. Score (%)	43.33%
Toppers Score (%)	66.67%
Your Score	

//Hints and Solutions//

1. Sulekha came to be called Bholi because she was not very intelligent.

"When she was ten months old, she had fallen off the cot on her head and perhaps it had damaged some part of her brain. That was why she remained a backward child and came to be known as Bholi, the simpleton."

Hence, the correct option is (A).

2. According to the passage, The smallpox attack do to Sulekha made her look ugly.

"But when she was two years old, she had an attack of smallpox. Only the eyes were saved, but the entire body was permanently disfigured by deep black pockmarks."

Hence, the correct option is (A).

3. According to the passage, Sulekha damaged her brain at ten months.

"When she was ten months old, she had fallen off the cot on her head and perhaps it had damaged some part of her brain."

Hence, the correct option is (A).

4. According to the passage, Bholi's mother agreed to send her to school because she wanted to wash her hands off Bholi.

"At last, his wife said, "I will tell you what to do. Send Bholi to school. As it is, there is little chance of her getting married, with her ugly face and lack of sense. Let the teachers at school worry about her."

Hence, the correct option is (A).

5. According to the passage, the statement, "She was healthy and strong" is not true about Bholi.

"Ramlal had seven children three sons and four daughters, and the youngest of them was Bholi. It was a prosperous farmer's household and there was plenty to eat and drink. All the children except Bholi were healthy and strong."

Hence, the correct option is (D).

6. The word 'disfigured' suggests that Bholi's looks were impaired.

Disfigured- spoil the attractiveness of

Impaired- weakened or damaged

Hence, the correct option is (B).

7. According to the passage, Ramlal was expected to set an example for the villagers by sending his daughters to school.

"He said to Ramlal, "As a revenue official you are the representative of the government in the village and so you must set an example to the villagers. You must send your daughters to school."

Hence, the correct option is (C).

8. According to the passage, Tehsildar was invited to inaugurate the girls' school.

The Tehsildar Sahib came to perform its opening ceremony. He said to Ramlal, "As a revenue official you are the representative of the government in the village and so you must set an example to the villagers. You must send your daughters to school."

Hence, the correct option is (C).

9. According to the passage, 'Backward child' in the passage means mentally challenged.

"When she was ten months old, she had fallen off the cot on her head and perhaps it had damaged some part of her brain. That was why she remained a backward child and came to be known as Bholi, the simpleton."

Hence, the correct option is (B).

10. According to the passage, Ramlal was worried about Bholi because it would be difficult to arrange her marriage.

"Of the daughters, Radha, the eldest, had already been married. The second daughter Mangla's marriage had also been settled, and when that was done, Ramlal would think of the third, Champa. They were good-looking, healthy girls, and it was not difficult to find bridegrooms for them. But Ramlal was worried about Bholi."

Hence, the correct option is (B).

11. According to the passage, Santiniketan initially served as a spiritual centre.

"In 1863, he turned it into a spiritual centre where people from all religions, castes and creeds came and participated in meditation."

Hence, the correct option is (C).

12. According to the passage, the statement, "Santiniketan was set up by Rabindranath Tagore" is not true about Santiniketan.

" In 1862, Maharishi Debendranath Tagore, father of Rabindranath, was taking a boat ride through Birbhum, the westernmost corner of Bengal, when he came across a landscape that struck him as the perfect place for meditation. He bought the large tract of land, built a small house, and planted some saplings. Debendranath Tagore decided to call the place Santiniketan, or the 'abode of peace, because of the serenity it brought to his soul."

Hence, the correct option is (D).

13. According to the passage, The curriculum designed for Santiniketan was a blend of human values, art and culture.

- "Blending the best of western and traditional eastern systems of education, the curriculum revolved organically around nature with classes being held in the open air."
- "Nature walks and excursions were a part of the curriculum, special attention was paid to natural phenomena and students were encouraged to follow the life cycles of insects, birds and plants."

Hence, the correct option is (C).

14. Tagore's 'erstwhile' home means former home.

Erstwhile: former or previous

Example: The border separated many schools and colleges from their erstwhile catchment areas.

Hence, the correct option is (B).

15. Rabindranath drop out of school because he felt stifled within the classroom.

" Tagore wanted his students to feel free despite being in the formal learning environment of a school because he himself had dropped out of school when he found himself unable to think and felt claustrophobic within the four walls of a classroom."

Hence, the correct option is (C).

16. Santiniketan was established to encourage education outside the classroom.

"Established in 1863 with the aim of helping education go beyond the confines of the classroom, Santiniketan grew into the Visva Bharati University in 1921, attracting some of the most creative minds in the country."

Hence, the correct option is (D).

17. The word 'unfettered' in the text suggests free from barriers.

Unfettered- unrestrained or uninhibited

Example: Poets are unfettered by the normal rules of sentence structure.

Hence, the correct option is (B).

18. Santiniketan grow into a university in 1921.

Look at the 2nd sentence from the first paragraph: "Established in 1863 with the aim of helping education go beyond the confines of the classroom, Santiniketan grew into the Visva Bharati University in 1921, attracting some of the most creative minds in the country."

Hence, the correct option is (C).

19. The name Santiniketan means abode of peace.

According to the passage, "Debendranath Tagore decided to call the place Santiniketan, or the 'abode of peace', because of the serenity it brought to his soul."

Hence, the correct option is (B).

20. Rabindranath was a 'formidable' literary force. This implies he was a powerful writer.

Formidable- causing you to have fear or respect for something or someone because that thing or person is large, powerful, or difficult.

Example: She was once a political nonentity but has since won a formidable reputation as a determined campaigner.

Hence, the correct option is (D).

21. The political decision making strategy has always taken the upper hand as compared to the real interests of the environment' has been attributed by the experts as a reason of the recent floods in Kerala and Karnataka.

Refer to, "Madhav Gadgil, who chaired the Union Environment Ministry's WGEEP, has said the recent havoc in Kerala is a consequence of short-sighted policymaking, and warned that Goa may also be in the line of nature's fury."

It is clear from the above that the experts are of the view that policy making has been the major reason of such floods in the country as it has not taken into account the environmental considerations of the area.

Hence, the correct option is (D).

22. The states should plan properly so that they can implement the recommendations of the expert panels regarding the preservation of the Western Ghats Area.

Refer to, "The State governments that are mainly responsible for the Western Ghats — Kerala, Karnataka, Tamil Nadu, Goa and Maharashtra — must go back to the drawing table with the reports of both the Gadgil Committee and the Kasturirangan Committee, which was set up to examine the WGEEP report. The task before them is to initiate correctives to environmental policy decisions."

It implies from the above lines that the states should ponder over the steps to be taken in order to preserve the ecology of the Western Ghats Area and they should think about implementation of the expert panel report on this issue.

Hence, the correct option is (C).

23. 'The balance between development and preservation should be there in order to develop the area properly' is the main issue pointed out in the passage in the implementation of the expert panel reports in various states.

Refer to, "This is not going to be easy, given the need to balance human development pressures with stronger protection of the Western Ghats ecology."

It is very much clear from the above lines that the objective of sustainable development is very difficult to meet with the political considerations in mind and that is why it becomes very difficult to strike a balance between the political objectives and the environmental requirements of the Western Ghats Area.

Option A is incorrect since the expert panel has recommended formation of committee and authority to oversee the development in the Western Ghats Area. Option B and C are not in sync with the given context though they may sound logical otherwise. Only Option D implies the same as has been depicted in the passage.

Hence, the correct option is (D).

24. 'The Western Ghats Area should be preserved properly so that there is sustainable development of the area' should be the objective of all concerned regarding the development of the Western Ghats Area.

Refer to, "The goal has to be sustainable development for the Ghats as a whole."

It is very clear that the main objective of all the activities surrounding the Western Ghats Area should be overall development of the region and also for all the parties concerned.

There should be sustainable development of all the regions in the area.

Except Option D, all the other options are not related to the given context and that is why they are eliminated. Option D implies the same as referred to in the above reference.

Hence, the correct option is (D).

25. Options I and III true should be the course of action of the government in order to ensure that the Western Ghats Area is preserved properly.

Refer to, "The role of big hydroelectric dams, built during an era of rising power demand and deficits, must now be considered afresh and proposals for new ones dropped. Other low-impact forms of green energy led by solar power are available. A moratorium on quarrying and mining in the identified sensitive zones, in Kerala and also other States, is necessary to assess their environmental impact."

It is clear that in order to preserve the Western Ghats Area, the solar energy should be promoted in the area along with moratorium on the mining and quarrying activities in the area. Apart from that, there should be restriction on construction of new hydroelectric power dams in the area.

Hence, the correct option is (C).

26. In the given passage it has been stated that Dr Kalam worked with three great minds. Dr. Vikram Sarabhai, of the Dept. of Space, Professor Satish Dhawan, who succeeded him and Dr. Brahm Prakash, father of nuclear material.

Hence, the correct option is (B).

27. The given passage is part of a speech given by Dr Kalam where he talks about his visions for India.

The second vision he has for India is with respect to development.

According to him, India spent 50 years as a developing nation and it is time that Indians saw themselves as a developed nation as India is among top five nations in the world in terms of GDP.

This is backed by the following sentences from the passage - 'For fifty years we have been a developing nation. It is time we see ourselves as a developed nation. We are among top five nations in the world in terms of GDP.'

Thus, we can infer that Dr Kalam wants every Indian to proclaim that India is a highly developed nation.

Hence, the correct option is (B).

28. Dr. Kalam feels that India should be strong in military power and economic power.

The given passage is part of a speech given by Dr Kalam where he talks about his visions for India. The third vision he has for India is with respect to strength. In the speech he states that -'We must be strong not only as a military power but also as an economic power.'

Hence, the correct option is (C).

29. The given passage is part of a speech given by Dr Kalam where he talks about his visions for India.

The first vision he has for India is with respect to freedom. The passage states that although India has been invaded by others time after time, India has not done the same to other countries. The passage states the reason behind this being - 'Because we respect the freedom of others.'

Thus, we can infer that respecting the freedom of others is one of the positive qualities that Indians have.

Hence, the correct option is (D).

30. The given passage is part of a speech given by Dr Kalam where he talks about his visions for India.

The second vision he has for India is with respect to development. In the passage Dr Kalam states - '... a developed nation, self-reliant and self-assured.' He urges the Indian population in his speech to work for the betterment of the country instead of expecting the nation to do everything for them.

Hence, the correct option is (C).

Ques (1-11):Direction: In the following question, out of the four alternatives, select the alternative which will improve the underlined part of the sentence. In case no improvement is needed, select "No improvement".

Q.1 In the major cities cost of life is very high.

A. cost of life are
B. the cost of living are
C. No improvement
D. the cost of living is

Q.2 The floods this year cause a lot of damage to the crops.

A. causing a lot of
B. cause lots of
C. have caused a lot of
D. No improvement

Q.3 I had to go to Delhi, however, I changed my mind and decided not to go.

A. therefore I change my mind
B. nevertheless I change my mind
C. however I will change my mind
D. No improvement

Q.4 If I had been there I would surely solve the problem for you.

A. I would surely have solved
B. I will surely solves
C. I would surely solving
D. No improvement

Q.5 Ajit has been played bridge since 2017.

A. is been playing bridge from 2017
B. has been play bridge from 2017
C. No improvement
D. has been playing bridge since 2017

Q.6 The news reported that the police have catched the guilty person and are interrogating him.

A. had caught the guilty
B. No improvement
C. have caught the guilty
D. are caught a guilty

Q.7 The watchman prevent him from parking his car near the gate.

A. prevents him for parking
B. prevented him to park
C. prevented him from parking
D. No improvement

Q.8 'Did you brought your drawing books?' the teacher asked the students.

A. Did you bring
B. Do you bringing
C. Do you brought
D. No improvement

Q.9 The children's cricket ball hit their neighbour's window and it broke.

A. and it is broke
B. and it broken
C. and it was breaking
D. No improvement

Q.10 The only vacant seat in the bus was right in the corner.

A. right on the corner
B. right into the corner
C. right up to the corner
D. No improvement

Q.11 Using seeds for grow more plants is an exceptionally good way of gardening.

A. No improvement
B. to growing more plants
C. to grow more plants
D. for grew more plants

Ques (12-30):Direction: In the following question, out of the four alternatives, select the alternative which will improve the underlined part of the sentence. In case no improvement is needed, select "No improvement".

Q.12 Unless Arjun takes a taxi he will not reach the airport in time.

A. However Arjun takes a taxi
B. If Arjun take a taxi
C. No improvement
D. Unless Arjun take taxi

Q.13 If you had intimated us about the arrival of guests, we would had made arrangements.

A. would have made
B. will have made
C. would have been made
D. No improvement

Q.14 They barely knew each other, do they?

A. did they
B. does they
C. didn't they
D. No improvement

Q.15 Shivam is going to meeting some of his friends, from his hometown, after work.

A. going meeting
B. going to meet
C. go to meet
D. No improvement

Q.16 Mohan cannot help bite his fingernails when he gets nervous.

A. cannot help to biting
B. cannot but help biting
C. cannot help biting
D. No improvement

Q.17 A lorry has shedded a load of gravel across the road.

A. shedded
B. have shed
C. has shed
D. No improvement

Q.18 The country's constitution was amended to allow women to vote.

A. emended **B.** amend
C. emends **D.** No improvement

Q.19 Since the holocaust took place, many innocent people lost their lives.

A. have been lost **B.** had lost
C. have lost **D.** No improvement

Q.20 None of the 14 firms are going to be sold by the government.

A. is going **B.** were going
C. have been going **D.** No improvement

Q.21 A retinue of about 70 persons have been entertaining in Italy at the pope's expense for 5 days.

A. has been entertaining
B. has being entertaining
C. is entertaining
D. No improvement

Q.22 If it won't rain tomorrow, we'll go to the Shopping Mall.

A. don't **B.** doesn't
C. isn't **D.** No improvement

Q.23 I love Radhika because she is a good girl by heart

A. at heart **B.** in heart
C. of heart **D.** No improvement

Q.24 They put the glass besides the book at the table.

A. beside the book at **B.** beside the book on
C. besides the book on **D.** No improvement

Q.25 Sneha agrees that her older brother is much clever than her.

A. her older brother is much clever to her
B. her elder brother is much clever to
C. her elder brother is much clever than
D. No improvement

Q.26 He behaved cowardly.

A. behaved in a cowardly manner
B. behaved in a coward manner
C. behave cowardly
D. No improvement

Q.27 You will not pass until you don't write accurately.

A. No improvement
B. till you write
C. unless you write
D. unless you don't write

Q.28 Mahima was tired as she was working since morning.

A. she has been working
B. she had been working
C. No improvement
D. she is working

Q.29 Farther discussion on the proposal will be deferred until August.

A. Further discussion on
B. Farther discussion of
C. Next discussion on
D. No improvement

Q.30 He is smarter enough to solve this problem.

A. smartest enough to **B.** smart enough of
C. smart enough to **D.** No improvement

// Smart Answer Sheet //

Correct Indicates percentage of students who answered questions correctly.

Skipped Indicates percentage of students who skipped questions.

Q.	Ans.	Correct	Skipped
1	D	43.15 %	45.81 %
2	C	44.99 %	54.07 %
3	D	67.68 %	32.23 %
4	A	42.13 %	38.02 %
5	D	63.14 %	32.59 %
6	C	53.79 %	30.24 %
7	C	56.01 %	40.55 %
8	A	63.33 %	31.94 %
9	D	54.77 %	42.27 %
10	D	66.14 %	33.62 %
11	C	52.3 %	46.26 %
12	C	45.31 %	30.79 %
13	A	51.55 %	42.36 %
14	A	63.96 %	30.2 %
15	B	67.06 %	30.49 %
16	C	45.21 %	31.33 %
17	C	59.27 %	39.48 %
18	D	49.19 %	30.78 %
19	C	65.15 %	31.23 %
20	A	44.02 %	46.35 %
21	A	47.89 %	40.54 %
22	B	64.44 %	34.55 %
23	A	56.83 %	30.19 %
24	B	45.4 %	38.12 %
25	C	58.48 %	38.96 %
26	A	60.09 %	37.79 %
27	C	53.71 %	38.14 %
28	B	58.87 %	34.7 %
29	A	60.04 %	31.27 %
30	C	62.76 %	32.36 %

Performance Analysis	
Avg. Score (%)	26.67%
Toppers Score (%)	53.33%
Your Score	

//Hints and Solutions//

1. 'Cost of life' is wrong usage. The right usage would be 'cost of living'.

Since, the subject of the be verb here' is 'cost', we have to use the singular form of the verb. Thus, neither options (A), nor (B) can be the answer to the question.

Hence, the correct option is (D).

2. The tense of the verb in the given sentence is incorrect.

We are talking about an event that happened in the current year. Thus, we have to use the present perfect form of the verb 'cause'.

So, the correct sentence is: The floods this year have caused a lot of damage to the crops.

Hence, the correct option is (C).

3. None of the phrases given in the options can be a substitute for the underlined part of the sentence in question.

Since, two conflicting events are taking place, we can't use 'therefore', as it puts emphasis on and follows the first event.

Nevertheless is an adverb which means 'in spite of' or 'despite'. It is used when one argument is especially strong.

Hence, the correct option is (D).

4. The first part of the sentence contains the past perfect form of the 'be' verb. The second part must agree with the tense present in the first part. Only option (A) has the required past perfect tense.

Hence, the correct option is (A).

5. When we refer to something that has been going on for quite some time, we use the present perfect continuous tense of the verb.

Only option (D) contains 'has been playing', the present perfect continuous tense.

Hence, the correct option is (D).

6. The correct form of the verb 'catch', when used with either the present perfect or the past perfect tense, is 'caught' (V_3).

So, the correct sentence would be:

The news reported that the police have caught the guilty person and are interrogating him.

Hence, the correct option is (C).

7. The correct sentence would be:

The watchman prevented him from parking his car near the gate.

In this case, the sentence talks about a particular event which occurred in the past.

Since, we have no idea about the time frame, we use simple past. The use of present tense is grammatically incorrect.

Hence, the correct option is (C).

8. The correct sentence is:

'Did you bring your drawing books?' the teacher asked.

The sentence is in the simple past tense. When we use the past form of the verb 'do', we have to use the present form of the following verb. Thus, 'did brought' is an incorrect usage.

Hence, the correct option is (A).

9. The given sentence is in simple past tense so we will use the past tense form of the verb i.e., broke.

With the past tense form of the verb, 'is' cannot be used.

Option (A) is making no sense.

Option (B) is grammatically incorrect.

Option (C) is in the past continuous tense.

Hence, the correct option is (D).

10. The sentence is correct.

When 'corner' means an interior angle formed by two meeting walls, we use the preposition in.

Example:

- The keys are lying in the corner of the room.

Into means expressing movement or action with the result that someone or something becomes enclosed or surrounded by something else.

Example:

- Put the bowl into the fridge.
- Up to means as far as.

Example:

- I could not reach up to the wall.

Here, 'in' is correct. It means- at a point within an area or space; within the shape of something; surrounded by something; into something; forming the whole or part of something.

Hence, the correct option is (D).

11. The use of the preposition 'for' with the base form of the verb i.e., grow is incorrect.

Instead of 'for', 'to' should be used.

'To' cannot be used with 'growing' as it is grammatically incorrect.

Hence, the correct option is (C).

12. 'Unless' is used to introduce the case in which a statement being made is not true or valid.

Unless means 'used to say what will or will not happen if something else does not happen or is not true; except if'.

Here it is used correctly as the speaker states that Arjun will not reach the airport in time except if he takes a taxi.

With a singular noun, the use of 'takes' is correct.

Correct sentence: Unless Arjun takes a taxi he will not reach the airport in time.

Hence, the correct option is (C).

13. Conditional sentences are statements discussing known factors or hypothetical situations and their consequences.

One of the structures is mentioned below:

This particular type is followed when something didn't happen as a certain condition wasn't fulfilled.

If + Subject + had + V_3 + object, Subject + Would have + V_3 + Object.

In the underlined part of the given question, 'would have made' will be used as per the rule given above.

Correct Sentence: If you had intimated us about the arrival of guests, we would have made arrangements.

Hence, the correct option is (A).

14. If the statement is negative, the question tag must be positive and vice versa.

But if any of these words are used, the question tag will be positive:

Hardly, Scarcely, seldom, rarely, barely.

In the underlined part of the given question, 'did they' will be used as per the rule given above.

Correct Sentence: They barely knew each other, did they?

Hence, the correct option is (A).

15. For events that will take place in the near future, Present Continuous Tense is used.

The structure is given below:

Subject + is/am/are + V_1 + ing + Object.

In the underlined part of the given question, 'going to meet' will be used as per the rule given above.

Correct Sentence: Shivam is going to meet some of his friends, from his hometown, after work.

Hence, the correct option is (B).

16. Let's have a look at the modal formations given below:

Can/could not help + V_1 + ing

Can/could not help + but + V_1

Both of the phrases mean to have a compulsion to do something that is too strong to ignore or avoid.

In the underlined part of the given question, 'cannot help biting' will be used as per the rule given above.

Correct Sentence: Mohan cannot help biting his fingernails when he gets nervous.

Hence, the correct option is (C).

17. The verbs given below have the same present, past, and past participle forms:

bid, cut, hurt, put, broadcast, shed, quit, spread, etc.

In the underlined part of the given question, 'has shed' will be used as per the rule given above.

Correct Sentence: A lorry has shed a load of gravel across the road.

Hence, the correct option is (C).

18. Let's look at the meanings of the given verbs:

amend- to improve (may be used in other contexts too)

emend- to remove the mistakes (for textual corrections)

Since a modification in the constitution is being talked about in the sentence, 'amended' will be the correct choice.

Correct Sentence: The country's constitution was amended to allow women to vote.

Hence, the correct option is (D).

19. Since can only be used with perfect tenses.

Example: We have taught at this school since 1965. They have been at the hotel since last Tuesday.

In the underlined part of the given question, 'have lost' will be used as per the rule given above, as it is a perfect tense.

Since 'be' form of the verb is not present in the latter part of the sentence we cannot use have been lost.

Correct Sentence: Since the holocaust took place, many innocent people have lost their lives.

Hence, the correct option is (C).

20. 'Neither/either of' is used when we have to choose between the two options.

Whereas 'None/one of' is used when we have to choose between more than two options.

In the underlined part of the given question, 'is going' will be used as per the rule given above.

Correct Sentence: None of the 14 firms is going to be sold by the government.

Hence, the correct option is (A).

21. In a sentence, the verb is used according to person and number.

Collective nouns take a singular verb with them.

In the underlined part of the given question, 'has been entertaining' will be used as per the rule given above.

Correct Sentence: A retinue of about 70 persons has been entertaining in Italy at the pope's expense for 5 days.

Hence, the correct option is (A).

22. Conditional sentences are statements discussing known factors or hypothetical situations and their consequences.

If two actions take place one after the other in the future, the structure will be as given below:

If + Subject + V_1 + Object, Subject + Will + V_1 + Object.

In the underlined part of the given question, 'doesn't' will be used as per the rule given above.

Correct Sentence: If it doesn't rain tomorrow, we'll go to the Shopping Mall.

Hence, the correct option is (B).

23. Here, in the given sentence the most appropriate substitution is 'at heart'.

We know that 'at heart' is 'used to say what someone is really like'.

Example: He had dozens of friends, but he was a private person at heart.

In the given sentence the girl 'Radhika' is loved by the person. Hence, the usage of 'at' with heart is correct.

Correct Sentence: I love Radhika because she is a good girl at heart.

Hence, the correct option is (A).

24. Beside means at the side of or next to.

For example:

- She sat beside her friend on the bus.
- They put the drinks beside the snacks on the table.

Besides means in addition to or apart from.

For example:

- She's capable of doing the work and a lot more besides.
- She didn't play with anybody else besides Ava.

After understanding the meanings of the words we can say 'beside' is the appropriate choice for the given phrase, as the glass is next to the book.

Also, If something is physically attached or joined to something else, then we use the preposition "on".

'At' is used for a point or for an enclosed space. Here, in the sentence drink is physically attached to that table so On should be used.

The correct sentence is: They put the glass beside the book on the table.

Hence, the correct option is (B).

25. 'Elder' and 'eldest' mean the same as 'older' and 'oldest'.

We only use the adjectives elder and eldest before a noun (as attributive adjectives), and usually when talking about relationships within a family.

Example: Let me introduce Siga. She's my elder sister.

Older and oldest can be used to refer to the age of things more generally. It can be used for both persons and things.

Example: The town hall is by far the oldest building in the whole region.

In the above-given sentence, Sneha is referring to one of her family members.

Therefore, 'older' should be replaced by 'elder'.

The correct sentence is: Sneha agrees that her elder brother is much clever than her.

Hence, the correct option is (C).

26. The word 'cowardly' is an adjective that means 'lacking courage'.

As adjectives (such as cowardly) are not used to modify verbs (such as behave), option (C) and (D) get eliminated.

'coward' is a noun and 'manner' is also a noun. As two nouns are not used together, option (B) also gets eliminated.'

There can be two ways to write this, 'behaved with cowardliness' and 'behaved in a cowardly manner'.

The correct sentence is: He behaved in a cowardly manner.

Hence, the correct option is (A).

27. Here, in the given sentence the most appropriate improvement is 'unless you write'.

We know that the word until is used in the context of time and roughly means before and up to the time.

Example: The photographs will be on exhibition until the end of the month.

Whereas, the word 'unless' is used in the context of a precondition and means if this condition is not met.

Example: They threatened to kill him unless he did as they asked.

We know that 'unless and until' does not take 'not' with it. They already consist of negative meaning.

Unless means something similar to 'if ... not' or 'except if'.

Adding 'not' with them makes it superfluous.

Correct Sentence: You will not pass unless you write accurately.

Hence, the correct option is (C).

28. Here, in the given sentence the most appropriate substitution is ''she had been working''.

The first part of the sentence 'Mahima was tired' is in the past indefinite tense.

The past perfect/ past perfect continuous and past indefinite tense is used to sequence events in the past to show which event happened first.

The action that occurred first is shown in the past perfect tense and the other one in the past indefinite.

Example:

- The music had already started when the curtains opened. (It means that the music started and then the curtains opened.)

Correct Sentence: Mahima was tired as she had been working since morning.

Hence, the correct option is (B).

29. 'Farther' and 'further' are comparative adverbs or adjectives.

Further: We use 'further' before a noun to mean 'extra', 'additional' or 'a higher level'.

Example: She's gone to a college of further education.

Farther: When used as an adjective, 'farther' describes when one object is more distant than the other, requiring a measurement of the distance from one common point to both objects.

Example: The red car is farther away than the blue car.

The given sentence talks about the additional discussion on a proposal.

Therefore, the usage of 'further' is the most appropriate answer in the given sentence.

The correct sentence is: Further discussion on the proposal will be deferred until August.

Hence, the correct option is (A).

30. 'Enough' can be used as both an adverb and as a determiner.

'Enough' as an adverb meaning 'to the necessary degree' goes after the adjective or adverb that it is modifying, and not before it as other adverbs do. It can be used both in positive and negative sentences.

'Enough' when used as an adverb, is preceded by a positive degree adjective or adverb.

Example:

- He is greater enough to command you. (Incorrect)
- He is great enough to command you. (Correct)

Therefore from the above explanation, it is clear that 'smarter' used is in the given sentence should be replaced by 'smart'.

The correct sentence is: He is smart enough to solve this problem.

Hence, the correct option is (C).

Q.1 Select the wrongly spelt word.
A. Embarrass **B.** Embrace
C. Embody **D.** Embelish

Q.2 Select the wrongly spelt word.
A. Booty **B.** Blosom **C.** Brood **D.** Boast

Q.3 Select the wrongly spelt word.
A. Bouquet **B.** Retaliate
C. Humiliation **D.** Sarcassm

Q.4 Select the wrongly spelt word.
A. Particular **B.** Impateint
C. Fortunate **D.** Thoroughly

Q.5 Identify the word that is misspelt.
A. Reality **B.** Multiple
C. Speciality **D.** Acomodate

Q.6 Select the wrongly spelt word.
A. Abhorrent **B.** Privarticate
C. Circuitous **D.** Finicky

Q.7 Select the correctly spelt word.
A. Equelibrium **B.** Equilriam
C. Equilibrium **D.** Equillibrium

Q.8 Select the wrongly spelt word.
A. Courtesy **B.** Diffedent
C. Sincerity **D.** Collapse

Q.9 Select the correctly spelt word.
A. Inchantment **B.** Ingagement
C. Installment **D.** Ingrediant

Q.10 Select the correctly spelt word.
A. Magnanemous **B.** Magnanomous
C. Magnanimous **D.** Magnonimus

Q.11 Select the correctly spelled word from the following.
A. Manuoeuvre **B.** Manoeuvre
C. Manoeuvere **D.** Maneoeuvre

Q.12 Select the correctly spelled word from the following.
A. Recalcetrant **B.** Recalcitrant
C. Recalcitrient **D.** Recalcitrent

Q.13 Select the correctly spelled word from the following.
A. Pirfidious **B.** Perfideous
C. Pirfideous **D.** Perfidious

Q.14 Choose the correctly spelt word from among the following words.
A. Intellegible **B.** Incomperable
C. Incidental **D.** Neglegible

Q.15 Choose the correctly spelt word from among the following words.
A. Punctelious **B.** Provedential
C. Precident **D.** Temperament

Q.16 A word is spelt in four different ways. Identify the one which is correct and mark your answer accordingly.
A. Mountaneous **B.** Mountenous
C. Mountaineous **D.** Mountainous

Q.17 A word is spelt in four different ways. Identify the one which is correct and mark your answer accordingly.
A. Etiquette **B.** Etiquete **C.** Etiequtte **D.** Etequtte

Q.18 A word is spelt in four different ways. Identify the one which is correct and mark your answer accordingly.
A. Magnificent **B.** Magnificant
C. Magneficent **D.** Magenficient

Q.19 A word is spelt in four different ways. Identify the one which is correct and mark your answer accordingly.
A. Neurasis **B.** Nuroesis **C.** Neurosis **D.** Neuresis

Q.20 A word is spelt in four different ways. Identify the one which is correct and mark your answer accordingly.
A. Dipththeria **B.** Diptheria
C. Diphtheria **D.** Diphthria

Q.21 A word is spelt in four different ways. Identify the one which is correct and mark your answer accordingly.
A. Meagre **B.** Megare **C.** Meagr **D.** Megear

Q.22 Select the wrongly spelt word.
[SSC Sub Inspector (CPO), 2020]
A. Supporting **B.** Easier
C. Difficult **D.** Optsion

Q.23 Select the wrongly spelt word.
[SSC Sub Inspector (CPO), 2020]
A. Pupil **B.** Capacity **C.** Teacher **D.** Ablity

Q.24 Select the wrongly spelt word.
[SSC Sub Inspector (CPO), 2020]
A. Occurring **B.** Exprimant
C. Sediment **D.** Umbrella

Q.25 Select the INCORRECTLY spelt word.
A. Existence **B.** Commitment
C. Distance **D.** Arguement

Q.26 Select the correctly spelt word from the given alternatives.
A. Cognizanse **B.** Cognezance
C. Cognizence **D.** Cognizance

Q.27 Select the incorrectly spelt word.

A. Occassion **B.** Violence
C. Fierce **D.** Resemblance

Q.28 Select the correctly spelt word from the given alternatives.

A. Cantankeruous **B.** Cantenkerous
C. Cantankarous **D.** Cantankerous

Q.29 Select the incorrectly spelt word.

A. Schedule **B.** Vacuum
C. Trenquility **D.** Acceleration

Q.30 Select the wrongly spelt word.

A. Session **B.** Satiate **C.** Settle **D.** Satallite

// Smart Answer Sheet //

Correct Indicates percentage of students who answered questions correctly.

Skipped Indicates percentage of students who skipped questions.

Q.	Ans.	Correct	Skipped
1	D	42.18 %	52.21 %
2	B	50.25 %	30.16 %
3	D	42.09 %	47.76 %
4	B	54.93 %	40.03 %
5	D	62.46 %	35.11 %
6	B	51.43 %	31.1 %
7	C	68.48 %	31.06 %
8	B	64.73 %	31.84 %
9	C	57.06 %	30.12 %
10	C	60.37 %	37.68 %
11	B	63.84 %	32.31 %
12	B	64.0 %	31.74 %
13	D	40.23 %	57.17 %
14	C	55.02 %	35.32 %
15	D	58.08 %	37.56 %
16	D	58.85 %	30.24 %
17	A	41.55 %	52.43 %
18	A	57.3 %	30.07 %
19	C	66.96 %	31.14 %
20	C	57.67 %	34.64 %
21	A	43.78 %	47.16 %
22	D	44.12 %	40.77 %
23	D	67.36 %	31.39 %
24	B	59.31 %	30.66 %
25	D	67.25 %	31.33 %
26	D	65.3 %	34.23 %
27	A	46.33 %	41.37 %
28	D	49.2 %	42.01 %
29	C	56.85 %	33.35 %
30	D	41.83 %	33.7 %

Performance Analysis	
Avg. Score (%)	63.33%
Toppers Score (%)	73.33%
Your Score	

//Hints and Solutions//

1. The correct spelling of Embelish is 'Embellish' which means 'to make something more beautiful by adding decoration to it'.

Embarrass: to make somebody feel shy, uncomfortable, or ashamed, especially in a social situation.

Embrace: an act of putting your arms around somebody as a sign of love or friendship.

Embody: to express or represent an idea or a quality.

Hence, the correct option is (D).

2. The correct spelling Blosom is "Blossom" which means mature or develop in a promising or healthy way.

Booty: valuable stolen goods, especially those seized in war.

Brood: a family of birds or other young animals produced at one hatching or birth.

Boast: an act of talking with excessive pride and self-satisfaction.

Hence, the correct option is (B).

3. The correct spelling of "Sarcassm" is "Sarcasm" which means speech or writing which actually means the opposite of what it seems to say. Sarcasm is usually intended to mock or insult someone.

Bouquet is a bunch of flowers that is attractively arranged.

Retaliate when someone harms or annoys you, you do something which harms or annoys them in return.

Humiliation is the embarrassment and shame you feel when someone makes you appear stupid, or when you make a mistake in public.

Hence, the correct option is (D).

4. Impateint is the wrongly spelt word. The correct word is Impatient. It means 'having or showing a tendency to be quickly irritated or provoked'.

Hence, the correct option is (B).

5. 'Acomodate' has been misspelt. The correct spelling is 'accommodate' and means (of a building or other area) provide lodging or sufficient space for.

Reality means the state of things as they actually exist, as opposed to an idealistic or notional idea of them.

Multiple means having or involving several parts, elements, or members.

Speciality means a pursuit, area of study, or skill to which someone has devoted much time and effort and in which they are expert.

Hence, the correct option is (D).

6. Privarticate is the wrongly spelt word. The correct word is Prevaricate. It means speak or act in an evasive way.

Hence, the correct option is (B).

7. Among all the given options, equilibrium is correctly spelt.

Equilibrium- a state in which opposing forces or influences are balanced

Hence, the correct option is (C).

8. Diffedent is the wrongly spelt word. The correct spelling is Diffident.

Diffident means modest or shy because of a lack of self-confidence.

Hence, the correct option is (B).

9. Installment is the correctly spelt word.

It means one of several parts into which a story, plan, or amount of money owed has been divided so that each part happens or is paid at different times until the end or total is reached.

Hence, the correct option is (C).

10. The correctly spelt word is 'Magnanimous'.

The meaning of the word 'Magnanimous' is 'charitable or generous'.

Hence, the correct option is (C).

11. The correctly spelled word out of the options is Manoeuvre which means "carefully guide or manipulate in order to achieve an end".

Example: The clutter of ships had little room to manoeuvre.

Hence, the correct option is (B).

12. The correctly spelled word out of the options is Recalcitrant which means "obstinately defiant of authority or restraint, having behaviour that is difficult to deal with".

Example: The teacher was fed up of his class of recalcitrant fifteen-year-olds.

Hence, the correct option is (B).

13. The correctly spelled word out of the options is Perfidious which means "showing no loyalty, deceitful and untrustworthy".

Example: You will not enjoy the fruits of your perfidious dealing.

Hence, the correct option is (D).

14. The correct spelt word is Incidental.

Incidental which means loosely associated, occurring by chance.

Hence, the correct option is (C).

15. The correctly spelt word is Temperament.

Temperament which means a person's usual manner of thinking, behaving or reacting.

Hence, the correct option is (D).

16. The correct answer is 'Mountainous.'

Mountainous': The correctly spelled word is 'Mountainous' and it means (of a region) having many mountains.

Example: The Antarctic is a mountainous area.

Hence, the correct option is (D).

17. The correct answer is 'Etiquette.'

'Etiquette': The correctly spelled word is 'Etiquette' and it means the customary code of polite behavior in society or among members of a particular profession or group.

Example: He refused to bow to the Queen, in deliberate breach of etiquette.

Hence, the correct option is (A).

18. The correct answer is 'Magnificent.'

'Magnificent': The correctly spelt word is 'Magnificent' and it means extremely beautiful, elaborate, or impressive.

Example: She looked magnificent in her wedding dress.

Hence, the correct option is (A).

19. The correct answer is 'Neurosis.'

'Neurosis': The correctly spelt word is 'Neurosis' and it means excessive and irrational anxiety or obsession.

Example: Behavior therapists believe that neurosis is learned and can be unlearned.

Hence, the correct option is (C).

20. The correct answer is 'Diphtheria.'

'Diphtheria': The correctly spelt word is 'Diphtheria' and it is a serious infection caused by strains of bacteria called Corynebacterium diphtheriae that make a toxin (poison).

Example: Europe now accounts for 80 percent of diphtheria cases reported worldwide.

Hence, the correct option is (C).

21. The correct answer is 'Meagre.'

'Meagre': The correctly spelt word is 'Meagre' and it means (of something provided or available) lacking in quantity or quality.

Example: Dietaries differed, here too ample, there meagre to starvation.

Hence, the correct option is (A).

22. 'Optsion: There is no such word in English or we can say that there is some spelling mistake in this word, the correct spelling is 'Option'.

'Option' means something that you can choose to do; the freedom to choose.

'Supporting' means giving assistance to someone or something.

'Easier' means without difficulty or effort.

'Difficult' means characterized by or causing hardships or problems.

Hence, the correct option is (D).

23. 'Ablity': There is no such word in English or we can say that there is some spelling mistake in this word, correct spelling is 'Ability'.

'Ability' means the mental or physical power or skill that makes it possible to do something.

'Pupil' is a person who is taught by another, especially a schoolchild or student in relation to a teacher.

'Capacity' means the maximum amount that something can contain.

'Teacher' is a person who teaches, especially in a school.

Hence, the correct option is (D).

24. 'Exprimant': There is no such word in English or we can say that there is some spelling mistake in this word, correct spelling is 'Experiment'.

'Occurring' means happening; taking place.

'Sediment' means matter that settles to the bottom of a liquid.

'Umbrella' is a device consisting of a circular canopy of cloth on a folding metal frame supported by a central rod, used as protection against rain.

Hence, the correct option is (B).

25. The correct spelling of 'Arguement' is ARGUMENT and it means an exchange of diverging or opposite views, typically a heated or angry one.

All other given options have been spelt correctly.

Hence, the correct option is (D).

26. Cognizance: awareness, realization, or knowledge, notice, perception.

When you have cognizance, you have knowledge of something.

Example: The guests took cognizance of the snide remark.
Hence, the correct option is (D).

27. The correct spelling is Occasion and it means "a particular event or the time at which it takes place."

The rest of the words are spelt correctly.

Their meanings are given below:

Violence: behaviour involving physical force intended to hurt, damage, or kill someone or something.

Fierce: having or displaying an intense or ferocious aggressiveness.

Resemblance: the state of resembling or being alike.

Hence, the correct option is (A).

28. Cantankerous: bad-tempered, argumentative, and uncooperative.

Someone who is cantankerous is always finding things to argue or complain about.

Hence, the correct option is (D).

29. The correct spelling is 'tranquility'.

Tranquillity means: a peaceful, calm state, without noise, violence, worry, etc.

Meaning of other words in the option are:

Schedule: A schedule is a plan that gives a list of events or tasks and the times at which each one should happen or be done.

Vacuum: If someone or something creates a vacuum, they leave a place or position which then needs to be filled by another person or thing.

Acceleration: The acceleration of a process or change is the fact that it is getting faster and faster.

Hence, the correct option is (C).

30. The correct word is Satellite- an artificial body placed in orbit around the earth or moon or another planet in order to collect information or for communication.

Meaning of the other words given in the option are:

Session: A session is a meeting of a court, parliament, or other official groups.

Satiate: If something such as food or pleasure satiates you, you have all that you need or all that you want of it, often so much that you become tired of it.

Settle: If something is settled, it has all been decided and arranged.

Hence, the correct option is (D).

Ques (1-20):Direction: Each question in this section has a sentence with three parts labelled (a), (b) and (c). Read each sentence to find out whether there is an error in any part and if you find no error, your response should be indicated as (d).

Q.1 He had arrived at Cairo (a)/ a few months before (b)/ protests shook the Arab world. (c)/ No error (d)

[UPSC NDA, 2019]

A. (a) **B.** (b) **C.** (c) **D.** (d)

Q.2 Most of us who are older competitive runners (a)/ are not able to race anywhere at the same speed (b)/ as we do when we were 30. (c)/ No error (d)

[UPSC NDA, 2019]

A. (a) **B.** (b) **C.** (c) **D.** (d)

Q.3 Work hard (a)/ lest you do not (b)/ fail. (c)/ No error (d)

[UPSC NDA, 2019]

A. (a) **B.** (b) **C.** (c) **D.** (d)

Q.4 The Eastern Ghats are home of 2600 plant species (a)/ and this habitat fragmentation (b) / can pose a serious threat to endemic plants. (c)/ No error (d)

[UPSC NDA, 2019]

A. (a) **B.** (b) **C.** (c) **D.** (d)

Q.5 Turbidity current is a fast-moving current (a)/ that sweeps down submarine canyons, (b)/ carrying sand and mud into the deep sea. (c)/ No error (d)

[UPSC NDA, 2019]

A. (a) **B.** (b) **C.** (c) **D.** (d)

Q.6 Everyone (a)/ of the boys (b)/ love to ride. (c)/ No error (d)

[UPSC NDA, 2019]

A. (a) **B.** (b) **C.** (c) **D.** (d)

Q.7 Neither praise nor blame (a)/ seem (b)/ to affect him. (c)/ No error (d)

[UPSC NDA, 2019]

A. (a) **B.** (b) **C.** (c) **D.** (d)

Q.8 Many a man (a)/ has succumbed (b)/ to this temptation. (c)/ No error (d)

[UPSC NDA, 2019]

A. (a) **B.** (b) **C.** (c) **D.** (d)

Q.9 A time slot of fifteen minutes (a)/ are allowed (b)/ for each speaker. (c)/ No error (d)

[UPSC NDA, 2019]

A. (a) **B.** (b) **C.** (c) **D.** (d)

Q.10 He asked (a)/ whether either of the brothers (b)/ were at home. (c)/ No error (d)

[UPSC NDA, 2019]

A. (a) **B.** (b) **C.** (c) **D.** (d)

Q.11 You don't have a (a)/ monopoly on suffering; (b)/ other people don't have problems too. (c)/ No error (d)

[UPSC NDA, 2021]

A. (a) **B.** (b) **C.** (c) **D.** (d)

Q.12 If you say that someone (a)/ you admire has feet of clay (b)/ you mean that they have hidden faults. (c)/ No error.(d)

[UPSC NDA, 2021]

A. (a) **B.** (b) **C.** (c) **D.** (d)

Q.13 He refused to change (a)/ his decision; (b)/ he refused it point out (c). No error. (d)

A. (a) **B.** (b) **C.** (c) **D.** (d)

Q.14 The importance of trade in Mughal times reinforced (a)/ the cultural definition of wealth as something (b)/ comprising of movable property. (c)/ No error (d)

[UPSC NDA, 2021]

A. (a) **B.** (b) **C.** (c) **D.** (d)

Q.15 In the nineteenth century, (a)/ most traditional scholars (b)/ tried to stay clear from the imperial Government. (c)/ No error (d)

[UPSC NDA, 2021]

A. (a) **B.** (b) **C.** (c) **D.** (d)

Q.16 He began his discussion by pointing over (a)/ that men and women (b)/ had different biological functions. (c)/ No error (d)

[UPSC NDA, 2021]

A. (a) **B.** (b) **C.** (c) **D.** (d)

Q.17 Though he is poor, (a)/ but he is (b)/ honest. (c)/ No error (d)

[UPSC NDA, 2021]

A. (a) **B.** (b) **C.** (c) **D.** (d)

Q.18 My mother (a)/ has been doing (b)/ everything for the family since day one. (c)/ No error (d)

[UPSC NDA, 2021]

A. (a) **B.** (b) **C.** (c) **D.** (d)

Q.19 When learning to dive (a)/ it is important(b)/ to relax in between and take breaks. (c)/ No error (d)

[UPSC NDA, 2021]

A. (a) **B.** (b) **C.** (c) **D.** (d)

Q.20 I have the opportunity (a)/ to study (b)/ in America next year. (c)/ No error(d)

[UPSC NDA, 2021]

A. (a) **B.** (b) **C.** (c) **D.** (d)

Ques (21-30):Direction: Each question in this section has a sentence with three parts labelled (A), (B) and (C). Read each sentence to find out whether there is an error in any part and if you find no error, your response should be indicated as (D).

Q.21 In emerging economies, the private credit market (A)/ remains highly segmented and thus (B)/ weaken the power of monetary policy. (C)/ No error (D)

A. (A) **B.** (B) **C.** (C) **D.** (D)

Q.22 Ten new members (A)/have been enrolled (B)/and seven have resigned. (C)/No error (D).

A. (A) **B.** (B) **C.** (C) **D.** (D)

Q.23 Wholesome strategic planning was the focus as (A)/ the firm manage through a difficult period (B)/ a couple of years ago. (C)/No error(D)

A. (A) **B.** (B) **C.** (C) **D.** (D)

Q.24 In spite of the best governmental efforts, (A)/ emission of green-house gases (B)/ and noxious chemicals remain a cause of worry. (C)/No error (D)

A. (A) **B.** (B) **C.** (C) **D.** (D)

Q.25 The rate of metabolism of (A)/ a body is comparatively lowest when (B)/ it is at rest and is thus optimum for examination. (C)/No error (D)

A. (A) **B.** (B) **C.** (C) **D.** (D)

Q.26 He'd have to wind up (A)/various affairs here on Moscow, (B)/ personal as well as business. (C)/No Error (D)

A. (A) **B.** (B) **C.** (C) **D.** (D)

Q.27 Danish has (A)/ ninety thousands (B)/ rupees only. (C)/ No error (D)

A. (A) **B.** (B) **C.** (C) **D.** (D)

Q.28 The eerie silence on the park (A)/ always reminded the children (B)/ of their trip to the wilderness. (C)/ No error (D)

A. (A) **B.** (B) **C.** (C) **D.** (D)

Q.29 An increase in the number (A) /of applicants raised the roof (B)/ for the students to get selected. (C)/ No error (D)

A. (A) **B.** (B) **C.** (C) **D.** (D)

Q.30 No man-made disaster(A)/ can surpass the fury of nature.(B)/ He is the most powerful.(C)/ No error(D)

A. (A) **B.** (B) **C.** (C) **D.** (D)

// Smart Answer Sheet //

Correct Indicates percentage of students who answered questions correctly.

Skipped Indicates percentage of students who skipped questions.

Q.	Ans.	Correct	Skipped
1	A	40.78 %	46.63 %
2	C	44.14 %	48.29 %
3	B	54.24 %	30.84 %
4	A	59.86 %	33.8 %
5	D	42.18 %	44.17 %
6	C	50.18 %	31.36 %
7	B	68.49 %	31.29 %
8	D	57.11 %	37.93 %
9	B	60.68 %	38.83 %
10	C	44.75 %	31.73 %
11	C	48.39 %	46.27 %
12	D	64.97 %	30.1 %
13	C	49.72 %	47.55 %
14	C	46.86 %	31.8 %
15	C	53.8 %	40.11 %
16	A	49.24 %	42.6 %
17	B	62.63 %	35.02 %
18	D	47.26 %	48.25 %
19	D	43.79 %	36.72 %
20	D	47.3 %	49.85 %
21	C	45.62 %	31.86 %
22	D	48.3 %	34.36 %
23	B	46.72 %	38.75 %
24	C	42.31 %	33.63 %
25	B	41.81 %	36.03 %
26	B	55.64 %	35.55 %
27	B	55.17 %	42.05 %
28	A	42.02 %	30.88 %
29	B	40.33 %	36.6 %
30	C	64.59 %	30.22 %

Performance Analysis	
Avg. Score (%)	36.67%
Toppers Score (%)	56.67%
Your Score	

//Hints and Solutions//

1. The main clause needs a simple past tense verb 'arrived', instead of the past perfect 'had arrived'.

Correct sentence: He arrived at Cairo a few months before protests shook the Arab world.

Hence, the correct option is (A).

2. In part (c) 'as we do when we were 30' has mixed tenses. (present followed by the past tense)

It should be - 'as we did when we were 30'.

Correct sentence: Most of us who are older competitive runners are not able to race anywhere at the same speed as we did when we were 30.

Hence, the correct option is (C).

3. In part (b) 'Lest' as the conjunction has a negative meaning. So, it cannot be used with another negative 'do not'.

The verb that always follows 'lest' is 'should'.

Correct sentence: Work hard lest you should fail.

Hence, the correct option is (B).

4. In part (a), 'home of' should be replaced with 'home to'.

'Home of' means a general term saying that usually, these plants live in such a habitat.

'Home to' means that currently, these plant species live in such a habitat.

Correct sentence: The Eastern Ghats is home to 2600 plant species and this habitat fragmentation can pose a serious threat to endemic plants.

Hence, the correct option is (A).

5. The sentence is grammatically correct. So, there is no need for correction.

Turbidity current is a fast-moving current that sweeps down submarine canyons, carrying sand and mud into the deep sea.

Hence, the correct option is (D).

6. Everyone shows that 'one' - a singular form of the boys - is indicated.

Thus, it requires a singular verb.

So, the verb will be 'loves'.

Correct sentence: Every one of the boys loves to ride.

Hence, the correct option is (C).

7. 'Neither, nor' conjunction joins two singular nouns 'praise and blame' - it needs a singular verb.

So, the verb in the given sentence should be singular - 'seems'.

Correct sentence: Neither praise nor blame seems to affect him.

Hence, the correct option is (B).

8. The sentence is grammatically correct. So, there is no need for correction.

Hence, the correct option is (D).

9. 'Each speaker' indicates a singular subject that needs a singular verb to agree with it 'is'.

In part (b), the verb is 'are' - a plural, which is incorrect.

Correct sentence: A time slot of fifteen minutes is allowed for each speaker.

Hence, the correct option is (B).

10. In part (c) 'were' will be replaced with 'was'.

'Either' is used to indicate 'one' or the other of two people or things.

So, it needs a singular verb 'was'.

Correct sentence: He asked whether either of the brothers was at home.

Hence, the correct option is (C).

11. Correct sentence: You don't have a monopoly on suffering; other people have problems too.

The error lies in Part (c) of the sentence.

The given sentence is not making complete sense.

Therefore, the use of 'Don't' in Part (c) of the sentence should be removed to make it grammatically correct.

Hence, the correct option is (C).

12. There is no error in the given sentences and it is providing a complete sense.

Correct sentence: If you say that someone you admire has feet of clay you mean that they have hidden faults.

Hence, the correct option is (D).

13. Correct sentence: He refused to change his decision; he refused to point it out.

- The error lies in Part (c) of the sentence.
- The given sentence is not making complete sense.
- A preposition 'to' should be used before the phrasal verb 'point out' in this context.
- Therefore, the use of 'it' in Part (c) of the sentence should be replaced with 'to' to make it grammatically correct.

Hence, the correct option is (C).

14. Correct sentence: The importance of trade in Mughal times reinforced the cultural definition of wealth as something comprised of movable property.

- The error lies in Part (c) of the sentence.
- The given sentence is not making complete sense.
- A preposition 'of' is used after the verb 'comprised.'

- Therefore, the use of 'comprising' in Part (c) of the sentence should be replaced with 'comprised' to make it grammatically correct.

Hence, the correct option is (C).

15. Correct sentence: In the nineteenth century, most traditional scholars tried to stay clear of the imperial Government.

- The error lies in Part (c) of the sentence.
- The meaning of the phrase 'clear of' is away from (something dangerous, harmful, etc.).
- Example: We'll pick up speed once we get clear of the heavy traffic.
- Therefore, the use of 'from' in Part (c) of the sentence should be replaced with 'of' to make it grammatically correct.

Hence, the correct option is (C).

16. Correct sentence: He began his discussion by pointing at that men and women had different biological functions.

- The error lies in Part (a) of the sentence.
- The meaning of the phrasal verb 'point at' is to show the position or direction of something by extending a finger or other pointed object towards it.
- Example: The librarian pointed at the sign that said to keep quiet.
- Therefore, the use of 'over' in Part (a) of the sentence should be replaced with 'at' to make it grammatically correct.

Hence, the correct option is (A).

17. Correct sentence: Though he is poor, he is honest.

- The error lies in Part (b) of the sentence.
- Since 'though' as subordinating conjunction implies or introduces a contrasting idea and 'but' as coordinating conjunction contrasts an idea.
- Both may go against the understanding that they negate each idea.
- Therefore, though and but are not used together if a comma (,) is present after the subordinate clause.
- Therefore, the use of 'but' in Part (b) of the sentence should be removed to make it grammatically correct.

Hence, the correct option is (B).

18. The given sentence is in Present Perfect Continuous Tense and the structure of the sentence is correct.

There is no error in the given sentences and it is providing a complete sense.

Hence, the correct option is (D).

19. Correct sentence: When learning to dive it is important to relax in between and take breaks.

There is no error in the given sentences and it is providing a complete sense.

Hence, the correct option is (D).

20. Correct sentence: I have the opportunity to study in America next year.

There is no error in the given sentences and it is providing a complete sense.

Hence, the correct option is (D).

21. Use 'weakens' in place of 'weaken'. The subject is singular so a singular verb is used.

Correct sentence: In emerging economies, the private credit market remains highly segmented and thus weakens the power of monetary policy.

Hence, the correct option is (C).

22. The given sentence is grammatically correct.

Ten new members have been enrolled and seven have resigned.

Hence, the correct option is (D).

23. Use 'managed' in place of 'manage' as the sentence is in the past tense.

Correct sentence: Wholesome strategic planning was the focus as the firm managed through a difficult period a couple of years ago.

Hence, the correct option is (B).

24. Use 'remains' in place of 'remain' as the subject is singular.

Correct sentence: In spite of the best governmental efforts, the emission of greenhouse gases and noxious chemicals remains a cause of worry.

Hence, the correct option is (C).

25. Use 'lower' in place of 'lowest' as a comparative degree is used after comparatively.

Correct sentence: The rate of metabolism of a body is comparatively lower when it is at rest and is thus optimum for examination.

Hence, the correct option is (B).

26. 'on' is incorrect, 'in' would be most appropriate.

For places we use, the preposition 'in'.

Correct sentence: He'd have to wind up various affairs here in Moscow, personal as well as business.

Hence, the correct option is (B).

27. Replace 'ninety thousands' with 'ninety thousand'. When a definite numeral adjective is added before the following nouns, they take singular form. The words are - Pair, score, gross, stone, hundred, dozen, thousand, million, billion, etc.

Example: She purchased three dozen pencils.

Correct sentence: Danish has ninety thousand rupees only.

Hence, the correct option is (B).

28. In the sentence, the phrase should be 'silence in the park' or 'silence around the park'. Therefore the first part is incorrect.

On preposition means physically in contact with and supported by (a surface).

Correct sentence: Silence around the park always reminded the children of their trip to the wilderness

Hence, the correct option is (A).

29. In the sentence, in the second part, the words used should have been 'raised the bar'.

Raised the bar means:

- To be better than what went before
- To raise standards or expectations
- To set higher rules/goals
- To make something harder

Correct sentence: An increase in the number of applicants raised the bar for the students to get selected.

Hence, the correct option is (B).

30. Nature should take the pronoun 'she' instead of 'he' as nature when personified is usually projected as feminine gender.

Correct sentence: No man-made disaster can surpass the fury of nature. She is the most powerful.

Hence, the correct option is (C).

Ques (1-6):Direction: Choose the word opposite in the meaning to the underlined word.

Q.1 The sky is boundless.

[UPSC NDA, 2021]

A. High **B.** Vast
C. Expansive **D.** Finite

Q.2 I have a fascination for deep waters.

[UPSC NDA, 2021]

A. Dark **B.** Light
C. Dangerous **D.** Shallow

Q.3 Spring is a time of plenty.

[UPSC NDA, 2021]

A. Ugliness **B.** Scarcity
C. Roughness **D.** Dryness

Q.4 He is an industrious workman.

[UPSC NDA, 2021]

A. Active **B.** Productive
C. Lazy **D.** Disloyal

Q.5 Plants grow in abundance here.

[UPSC NDA, 2021]

A. Shrivel **B.** Stretch **C.** Spread **D.** Enlarge

Q.6 She is a rather crooked woman.

[UPSC NDA, 2021]

A. Polite **B.** Generous
C. Straightforward **D.** Happy

Q.7 Direction: Choose the word similar in the meaning to the underlined word:

Few actors are as versatile as he is; he writes scripts, directs, and produces.

A. multi-purpose
B. greedy
C. having no specific interest
D. ambitious

Q.8 Direction: Select the most appropriate synonym of the given word.

SUMMON

A. call for **B.** dismiss **C.** order **D.** appear

Q.9 Direction: Select the synonym of the given word.

AFFINITY

A. Monotony **B.** Beauty
C. Empathy **D.** Decency

Q.10 Direction: Select the synonym of the given word.

STRAY

A. Slight **B.** Wander
C. Steady **D.** Gruesome

Q.11 Direction: Select the synonym of the given word.

ADULTERATED

A. Combined **B.** Fused
C. Contaminated **D.** Concentrated

Q.12 Direction: Select the most appropriate synonym of the given word.

SPONTANEOUS

[SSC Sub Inspector (CPO), 2020]

A. planned **B.** prejudiced
C. intended **D.** impulsive

Q.13 Direction: Select the most appropriate synonym of the given word.

DESOLATE

[SSC Sub Inspector (CPO), 2020]

A. cultivated **B.** protected
C. barren **D.** inhabited

Q.14 Direction: Select the most appropriate antonym of the given word.

IGNITE

[SSC Sub Inspector (CPO), 2020]

A. extinguish **B.** kindle
C. burn **D.** light

Q.15 Direction: Select the most appropriate synonym of the given word.

PRODIGAL

[SSC Sub Inspector (CPO), 2020]

A. modest **B.** intelligent
C. talented **D.** wasteful

Q.16 Direction: Select the most appropriate antonym of the given word.

IRRELEVANT

[SSC Sub Inspector (CPO), 2020]

A. immaterial **B.** trivial
C. pointless **D.** consequential

Q.17 Direction: Select the most appropriate synonym of the given word.

BENIGN

[SSC Sub Inspector (CPO), 2020]

A. severe **B.** malignant
C. favourable **D.** harsh

Q.18 Direction: Select the most appropriate synonym of the given word.

CHASTE

A. liberated **B.** divine **C.** defiled **D.** pure

Q.19 Direction: Select the most appropriate antonym of the given word.

EXONERATE

A. vindicate **B.** acquit **C.** sentence **D.** absolve

Ques (20-21):Direction: In the sentence, a word is underlined followed by four words/groups of words. Select the option that is nearest in meaning to the underlined word and Choose the correct option.

Q.20 The properties of the family have been <u>impounded</u> by the order of the court.

A. Confiscated **B.** Permitted
C. Sold **D.** Put on hold

Q.21 The manner in which this exercise has been undertaken leaves much to be <u>desired</u>.

A. Dislike **B.** Unlikely
C. Wish for **D.** Asked for

Ques (22-26):Direction: In the sentence, a word is underlined followed by four words/groups of words. Select the option that is opposite in meaning to the underlined word and Choose the correct option.

Q.22 Reading details about suicide cases can push <u>vulnerable</u> people to take the extreme step.

A. Imperious **B.** Impervious
C. Helpless **D.** Defenseless

Q.23 Standing before a judge in a courtroom can be <u>daunting</u> for anyone.

A. Uncomfortable **B.** Encouraging
C. Demoralizing **D.** Off-putting

Q.24 He has been facing a kind of <u>intimidation</u> by his friends for last two years.

A. Wiles **B.** Conviction
C. Persuasion **D.** Support

Q.25 People look for <u>plausible</u> remedies to the problems which they do not know.

A. Acceptable **B.** Unthinkable
C. Solvable **D.** Believable

Q.26 The members have taken a unanimous decision to <u>discord</u> some of the rulings of the Managing Committee on problems relating to maintenance.

A. Accord **B.** Dissension
C. Discript **D.** Dispute

Q.27 Direction: Select the most appropriate antonym of the given word.

PUNITIVE

A. Damaging **B.** Rewarding
C. Solvable **D.** Believable

Q.28 Direction: In the sentence, a word is underlined followed by four words/groups of words. Select the option that is opposite in meaning to the underlined word and Choose the correct option.

The <u>insolent</u> nature of the speaker had provoked the members of the house and this led to pandemonium.

A. Respectful **B.** Autocratic
C. Impudent **D.** Thought provoking

Ques (29-30):Direction: Select the most appropriate synonym of the underlined word.

Q.29 The poems of Kabir are <u>ecstatic</u> in nature.

A. Efficacious **B.** Eerie
C. Rapturous **D.** Reverential

Q.30 Massive

A. Lump sum **B.** Little
C. Gaping **D.** Huge

// Smart Answer Sheet //

Correct Indicates percentage of students who answered questions correctly.

Skipped Indicates percentage of students who skipped questions.

Q.	Ans.	Correct	Skipped
1	D	41.42 %	55.04 %
2	D	47.34 %	41.27 %
3	B	60.62 %	38.77 %
4	C	57.8 %	33.29 %
5	A	47.51 %	33.5 %
6	C	59.12 %	32.12 %
7	A	69.22 %	30.34 %
8	A	50.08 %	38.92 %
9	C	55.78 %	39.4 %
10	B	57.1 %	37.73 %
11	C	54.25 %	41.06 %
12	D	55.53 %	38.69 %
13	C	56.71 %	34.11 %
14	A	50.77 %	42.17 %
15	D	49.04 %	43.67 %
16	D	68.54 %	30.51 %
17	C	44.66 %	53.93 %
18	D	66.89 %	30.58 %
19	C	50.41 %	40.09 %
20	A	66.51 %	32.15 %
21	B	43.1 %	35.86 %
22	B	58.16 %	35.03 %
23	B	61.15 %	31.42 %
24	C	47.39 %	36.73 %
25	B	62.57 %	35.16 %
26	A	57.98 %	39.67 %
27	B	45.15 %	36.18 %
28	A	64.66 %	34.39 %
29	C	41.92 %	38.38 %
30	D	69.76 %	30.16 %

Performance Analysis	
Avg. Score (%)	53.33%
Toppers Score (%)	63.33%
Your Score	

//Hints and Solutions//

1. The word 'finite' is the opposite of the meaning of the underlined word 'boundless'.

The meaning of the given words:

- Boundless: unlimited, infinite or immense.
- Finite: limited in size or extent.
- High: great, or greater than normal, in quantity, size, or intensity.
- Vast: of very great extent or quantity, immense.
- Expansive: covering a wide area in terms of space or scope; extensive.

Hence, the correct option is (D).

2. The word 'shallow' is the opposite of the meaning of the underlined word 'deep'.

The meaning of the given words:

- Deep: extending far down from the top or surface.
- Shallow: of little depth.
- Dark: with little or no light.
- Light: having a considerable or sufficient amount of natural light; not dark.
- Dangerous: able or likely to cause harm or injury.

Hence, the correct option is (D).

3. The word 'scarcity' is the opposite of the meaning of the underlined word 'plenty'.

The meaning of the given words:

- Plenty: a situation in which food and other necessities are available in sufficiently large quantities.
- Scarcity: the state of being scarce or in short supply, shortage.
- Ugliness: the quality of being unpleasant or repulsive in appearance.
- Roughness: the quality or state of having an uneven or irregular surface.
- Dryness: absence or lack of moisture or liquid.

Hence, the correct option is (B).

4. The word 'lazy' is the opposite of the meaning of the underlined word 'industrious'.

The meaning of the given words:

- Industrious: diligent and hard-working.
- Lazy: unwilling to work or use energy.
- Active: engaging or ready to engage in physically energetic pursuits.
- Productive: producing or able to produce large amounts of goods, crops, or other commodities.
- Disloyal: failing to be loyal to a person, country, or organization to which one has obligations.

Hence, the correct option is (C).

5. The word 'shrivel' is the opposite of the meaning of the underlined word 'grow'.

The meaning of the given words:

- Grow: (of a living thing) undergo natural development by increasing in size and changing physically.
- Shrivel: wrinkle and contract or cause wrinkle and contract, especially due to loss of moisture.
- Stretch: to spread over a large area or distance.
- Spread: extend over a large or increasing area.
- Enlarge: make or become larger or more extensive.

Hence, the correct option is (A).

6. The word 'straightforward' is the opposite of the meaning of the underlined word 'crooked'.

The meaning of the given words:

- Crooked: dishonest
- Straightforward: uncomplicated and easy to do or understand, honest.
- Polite: having or showing behaviour that is respectful and considerate of other people.
- Generous: showing a readiness to give more of something, especially money, than is strictly necessary or expected.
- Happy: feeling or showing pleasure or contentment.

Hence, the correct option is (C).

7. The correct answer is Option 1 i.e., multi-purpose.

Versatile- able to adapt or be adapted to many different functions or activities.

Example: A leather jacket is a timeless and versatile garment that can be worn in all seasons.

Hence, the correct option is (A).

8. Of the given options, the only word that is similar in meaning is 'call for' which means to summon or request someone or something.

The word 'summon' is a verb that means order someone to be present.

- For eg: They were summoned to the court to give advice
- For eg: As I neared home, I could hear my mother calling for me.

Hence, the correct option is (A).

9. The word 'Affinity' means sympathy marked by community of interest.

The synonyms of the word 'Affinity' are "empathy, attraction, connection".

The word 'Empathy' means the ability to understand and share the feelings of another.

Hence, the correct option is (C).

10. Let's look at the meaning of the given word and the marked option:

- Stray - to wander from company, restraint, or proper limits
- Wander - to move about without a fixed course, aim, or goal

Thus, from the given meanings, we find that wander is the synonym for stray.

Let's look at the meanings of the other given options:

- Slight - having a slim or delicate build
- Steady - showing little variation or fluctuation
- Gruesome - inspiring horror or repulsion

Hence, the correct option is (B).

11. Let's look at the meaning of the given word and the marked option:

- Adulterated - weakened or lessened in purity by the addition of a foreign or inferior substance or element.
- Contaminated - made unfit for use by the introduction of unwholesome or undesirable elements.

Thus, from the given meanings, we find that Contaminated is the synonym for Adulterated.

Let's look at the meanings of the other given options:

- Combined - a skiing competition combining two separate events.
- Fused - to blend thoroughly by or as if by melting together.
- Concentrated - rich in respect to a particular or essential element.

Hence, the correct option is (C).

12. The correct answer is 'impulsive'.

The word 'Spontaneous' means done instantly and without conscious thought or decision.

Example: His jokes seemed spontaneous, but were in fact carefully prepared beforehand.

The synonyms of the word 'Spontaneous' are "impulsive, random, instinctive".

The word 'impulsive' means acting or done without forethought.

Example: He needs to learn to control his impulsive behavior.

Hence, the correct option is (D).

13. The word 'Desolate' means causing or marked by an atmosphere lacking in cheer.

Example: He is living in a desolate house abandoned many years ago.

The synonyms of the word 'Desolate' are "barren, bleak, cheerless, depressing".

From the synonym of the given word, we can say that the word 'barren' is the same in meaning.

The word 'barren' means lacking in cheer.

Example: The site of the town is a barren , rocky mountain valley.

Hence, the correct option is (C).

14. The correct answer is 'extinguish'.

The word 'Ignite' means to set something on fire.

Example: The fire was ignited by sparks.

The antonyms of the word 'Ignite' are "extinguish, put out".

From the antonym of the given word, we can say that the word 'extinguish' is opposite in meaning.

The word 'extinguish' means to cause to cease burning.

Example: he fire department was called in to extinguish the blaze.

Hence, the correct option is (A).

15. The correct answer is 'wasteful'.

The word 'Prodigal' means given to spending money freely or foolishly.

Example: The prodigal guys always spend their allowance the minute they get it.

The synonyms of the word 'Prodigal' are "wasteful, extravagant, squandering".

From the synonym of the given word, we can say that the word 'wasteful' is the same in meaning.

The word 'wasteful' means given to spending money freely or foolishly.

Example: Apart from being wasteful , just removing the old Exchange servers may have unpleasant side-effects.

Hence, the correct option is (D).

16. The correct answer is 'consequential'.

The word 'Irrelevant' means not connected with or relevant to something.

Example: He deletes what strikes him as irrelevant or tedious or uninteresting to his readers.

The antonyms of the word 'Irrelevant' are "consequential, meaningful, significant".

From the antonym of the given word, we can say that the word 'consequential' is opposite in meaning.

The word 'consequential' means of or at a fairly low temperature.

Example: The report discusses a number of consequential matters that are yet to be decided.

Hence, the correct option is (D).

17. The correct answer is 'favourable'.

The word 'Benign' means not harsh or stern, especially in nature or effect.

Example: They are normally a more benign audience.

The synonyms of the word 'Benign' are "favourable, gentle, peaceful".

From the synonym of the given word, we can say that the word 'favourable' is the same in meaning.

The word 'favourable' means promoting or contributing to personal or social well-being.

Example: My first impression of him was favourable.

Hence, the correct option is (C).

18. The correct answer is 'pure'.

The word 'Chaste' means free from any trace of the coarse or indecent.

Example: People in some religious orders remain chaste.

The synonyms of the word 'Chaste' are "pure, modest, clean".

From the synonym of the given word, we can say that the word 'pure' is the same in meaning.

The word 'pure' means free from any trace of the coarse or indecent.

Example: It is very difficult to know if the honey is pure.

Hence, the correct option is (D).

19. The correct answer is 'sentence".

The word 'Exonerate' means to free from a charge of wrongdoing.

Example: She was exonerated from the accusation of cheating.

The antonyms of the word 'Exonerate' are "sentence, accuse, convict".

From the antonym of the given word, we can say that the word 'sentence' is the opposite in meaning.

The word 'sentence' means the punishment assigned to a defendant found guilty by a court or fixed by law for a particular offence.

Example: He typed a short sentence , and then stopped.

Hence, the correct option is (C).

20. Impounded: to not let somebody use something by taking it away from them, especially because they have broken the law, seized and taken legal custody of something, especially a vehicle, goods or documents because of infringement of a law.

For example: He recovered all the immense grants of crown lands and rents, impounded by the nobles during his minority.

Confiscated: to take something away from somebody as a punishment.

For example: All Biren's vast property was confiscated , including his diamonds, worth millions.

Hence, the correct option is (A).

21. The correct answer is 'Impervious'.

Vulnerable: exposed to the possibility of being attacked or harmed, either physically or emotionally.

For example: Children are the most vulnerable members of society.

Impervious: unable to be affected or influenced by something.

For example: He clasped his arms behind his head and lay down, impervious to the cold.

Hence, the correct option is (B).

22. The correct answer is Impervious.

Vulnerable: exposed to the possibility of being attacked or harmed, either physically or emotionally.

For example: Children are the most vulnerable members of society.

Impervious: unable to be affected or influenced by something.

For example: He clasped his arms behind his head and lay down, impervious to the cold.

Hence, the correct option is (B).

23. The correct answer is Encouraging.

Daunting: seeming difficult to deal with in prospect; intimidating.

For example: As our activities grew, the task became more daunting.

Encouraging: giving someone support or confidence; supportive.

For example: Her parents said some encouraging words to cheer her up.

Hence, the correct option is (B).

24. The correct answer is Persuasion.

Intimidation: the action of intimidating someone, or the state of being intimidated, frightened, or scared.

For example: She then rashly tried intimidation and threatened to espouse the cause of Britannicus.

Persuasion: the action or process of persuading someone or of being persuaded to do or believe something.

For example: I had to use a little gentle persuasion to get her to agree.

Hence, the correct option is (C).

25. The correct antonym of plausible is unthinkable.

Plausible: (of an argument or statement) seeming reasonable or probable, that you can believe.

For example: She could find no plausible explanation for its disappearance.

Unthinkable: (of a situation or event) too unlikely or undesirable to be considered a possibility.

For example: The relation between cause and effect is unthinkable.

Hence, the correct option is (B).

26. The correct antonym of discord is accord.

Discord: disagreement between people; lack of harmony between notes sounding together.

For example: A few years later discord arose among the allies.

Accord: give or grant someone (power, status, or recognition); an official agreement or treaty especially between countries.

For example: He decided to go of his own accord

Hence, the correct option is (A).

27. The correct antonym of punitive is rewarding.

Punitive: intended as a punishment

Rewarding: giving satisfaction; making you happy because you think it is important, useful, etc.

Damaging: to affect injuriously.

Solvable: susceptible of solution or of being solved, resolved, or explained.

Believable: capable of being believed especially as within the range of known possibility or probability.

Hence, the correct option is (B).

28. The correct answer is respectful.

Insolent: showing a rude and arrogant lack of respect.

For example: They were extremely insolent to the police officers who tried to get them to leave.

Respectful: feeling or showing deference and respect.

For example: The children in our family are always respectful to their elders.

Hence, the correct option is (A).

29. The option that is nearest in meaning to the underlined word ' ecstatic' is 'rapturous'.

Ecstatic means feeling or expressing overwhelming happiness or joyful excitement.

Rapturous means characterized by, feeling, or expressing great pleasure or enthusiasm.

Hence, the correct option is (C).

30. Synonym of Massive is Huge.

Lump sum : a single payment made at a particular time, as opposed to a number of smaller payments or installments.

Little : small in size, amount, or degree.

Gaping : wide open.

Huge : extremely large; enormous.

Massive : exceptionally large.

Hence, the correct option is (D).

// Notes //

// Notes //

www.ingramcontent.com/pod-product-compliance
Ingram Content Group UK Ltd.
Pitfield, Milton Keynes, MK11 3LW, UK
UKHW061704190726
13853UKWH00008B/2402

9 789355 561749